A PSYCHIC WITCH SUPERNATURAL MYSTERY

Peppermint and Potions

THE TEA SHOP WITCH
COZY MYSTERY SERIES BOOK TWO

THORA BLUESTONE

Book Description

Addie James's attempts to help out in Aunt Kate's tea shop are about to backfire bigtime, and Addie's new magic won't be enough to get her out of a murder charge.

Somewhat settled in the idyllic mountain town of Stargaze, former scientist Addie James still isn't sure what she's going to do with her life—or her newly discovered magical talent for reading tea leaves. In the meantime, she's helping out at her Aunt Kate's shop, Wild Rose Teas and Apothecary.

But after buying an herbal remedy Addie made, the mayor's wife turns up dead. Addie is the prime suspect!

Now she must beat the clock and use her newfound magic to find the true killer before she'll be forced to sit trial for murder. But there's one big problem: things like tea leaf readings don't exactly provide the type of evidence the authorities are interested in. It's going to take more than magic to keep Addie from a life sentence.

Books by Thora Bluestone

<u>The Tea Shop Witch Cozy Mysteries</u>

The Tea Shop Witch (#1)

Peppermint and Potions (#2)

Chamomile and Crystal Balls (#3)

Bergamot and Brains (#4)

Vanilla and Vampires (#5)

Go to www.ThoraBluestone.com/newsletter to sign up for subscriber-only updates, deals, freebies, and news from Thora!

Contents

Chapter One

ADDIE JAMES HELD THE AMBER glass dropper bottle in her hand, squinted, and concentrated on channeling magic.

She really was trying, but it wasn't going great. In fact, nothing at all seemed to be happening.

She squinted harder and tried to block out everything else, funneling her focus down to just the glass bottle.

Concentrate, concentrate, concentrate.

The thing was, she wasn't totally sold on the existence of magic. That made it a little hard to not feel conflicted.

Even though she'd used tea-leaf divination, also called tasseomancy or tasseography, to help catch the man who'd nearly killed her Aunt Kate, Addie still wasn't on board with the whole supernatural abilities business.

"Let your intention flow through you," Kate instructed quietly. "Intention is at the root of every witch's magic."

Addie winced at her aunt's words.

Witch.

She just couldn't think of herself as a witch.

Shaking her head, she set the bottle on the counter under the shelves of Kate's shop, Wild Rose Teas and Apothecary.

"I'm sorry, Aunt Kate," Addie said. "I just can't seem to figure out how to do what you're asking."

Kate smiled, tilted her head, and patted Addie's hand. "It takes practice."

Addie happened to glance down and caught a glimpse of the strip of Kate's wrist that was exposed by a slightly pulled-up sleeve. Kate had covered the backs of her hands in tinted foundation to mask the pale pea-green pallor of her skin but hadn't extended the makeup up to her wrists.

Aunt Kate was, well . . .

A Shuffler. Reanimated. *Zombie.*

It was still hard to believe that zombies existed and that Addie's aunt was one of them. She still mostly looked like the Aunt Kate Addie remembered, but Kate was no longer human.

"How much longer can you stay today?" Addie asked hopefully.

Still new to living in Stargaze, Oregon, she'd been manning Wild Rose Teas and Apothecary every day for the past few weeks, enabling her aunt to keep the beloved business open while she adjusted to her new life as a Shuffler. As a brand-new zombie, Kate wasn't allowed to stay within the human population for more than a few hours at a time. She was still learning to recognize and control her hunger urges, but it took time. And in the meantime, she could be a danger to humans if she lost control. That meant living in an area of west Stargaze she referred to as Shuffleville.

"Gosh, I probably only have another hour or so in me," Kate said. She leaned against the counter, looking glassy-eyed and tired.

Addie's heart sank a little at that, but she reminded herself that Kate was doing her best.

Addie reached under the register, pulled out a bottle of eyedrops, and passed them to her aunt. Red-rimmed, bloodshot eyes were another hallmark of zombieism.

"Thanks," Kate said and tipped her head back to squirt a couple of drops in each eye. "I know you wish I could stay longer. I do, too."

Addie ran a hand over her hair and sighed. "It's just ... I'm clearly not capable of giving your apothecary clients what they've come to expect from you. Not without being able to, you know . . ."

"I still believe you'll learn how to perform herbal magic," Kate said.

She tried for a smile, but Addie saw the shadow of sadness behind it. Apparently, Kate's transformation had taken away her magic. They both still hoped that with time it might return, but so far there was no sign of it. So, in the meantime, Kate was trying to teach Addie the "special sauce" that Wild Rose Teas and Apothecary was known for—the magical ingredient that made Kate's remedies so powerfully curative.

"But even without the magic," Kate continued. "My clients—-*our* clients—are still getting high quality remedies that help them immensely."

Addie didn't have a chance to respond, as the door swung open and two women came in. One was older and sat on a powered scooter. The other was about Kate's age and with the longest, fluffiest hair Addie had ever seen. It hung past the waist of the woman's jeans, and there was almost an ethereal quality to the way the strawberry-blond mass drifted when she moved.

So entranced by the hair of the younger one, it took Addie a moment to recognize that the women had to be related. They had the same deep-set brown eyes and square chin.

The younger woman seemed to be hiding her annoyance behind her hard-pressed lips while she waited for the older woman to maneuver through the doorway.

". . . and that mayor's wife, I'll tell you what," the older woman was saying. "She's got it out for us, and I'm not going to stand for it. She's not going to get away with it. I promise you that right now."

"Hush, Mama," the younger one murmured.

"Edna. Heather. What can I do for you today?" Kate greeted them cheerfully. But Addie could tell by her aunt's forced smile that these women weren't her favorite customers.

"Oh, well, you know I have so many challenges," the older woman said as she scooted toward the counter. "I'm just here for refills."

"The gout's still bad, Edna?" Kate asked.

"Oh, yes," Edna said, her head beginning to nod rhythmically as she started reciting a list of aliments. "The gout, the palpitations, the constipation, the anxiety, the arthritis, the insomnia, the dizziness—"

"Mama," the younger woman cut in quietly. "That's quite enough, now." She offered a strained, apologetic smile to Kate.

"No worries, Edna, I've got all of your remedies right here," Kate said, tapping a finger on the spiral-bound notebook next to the register. "Why don't the two of you have a seat? My niece Addie, here, will bring you some nice mint tea while you wait for the formulations."

Edna squinted, her face taking on a pained expression.

"The tea is on the house," Kate said.

"Oh, well then, that would be delightful," Edna said, her face relaxing.

Addie made a pot of mint tea while Kate gathered the various tinctures for Edna's remedies.

When Addie took the pot and two mugs to the table where Heather sat in a chair and Edna remained on her scooter, the mother and daughter seemed to be engaged in a quiet argument.

Addie didn't intentionally try to overhear but couldn't help picking up some of the conversation as she poured the tea.

". . . and if you think I can handle that on my own, well, you're blind and not terribly bright," Edna was saying. She pushed out her lower lip in a pout.

"Mama, I'm not abandoning you or the store," Heather said. "I'd like to close for that day. It's just one day."

"And what would our customers think of that?" Edna shook her head in disgust.

Instead of responding, Heather cast Addie a tight smile.

Addie went to rejoin Kate at the apothecary counter.

"Are they usually like that?" Addie whispered.

Kate nodded. "I've always felt sorry for Heather. Edna's got her on such a tight leash the poor woman doesn't have a life of her own. It's sad, really."

"Edna mentioned a store."

"They have a donut shop downtown, Glazed."

"Oh, I remember that place from when I was a kid," Addie said. "But didn't an older couple own it?"

"They did, but they sold it to Edna and Heather a few years back."

For the next several minutes, Kate instructed Addie in preparing half a dozen different tinctures. Addie went through the motions of trying to instill them with magic, following the steps Kate described, but didn't feel the inner spark that was supposedly evidence of Kate's "special sauce."

"I think you're close," Kate said, patting Addie's hand.

But Addie suspected Kate was just being nice about it. Addie was seriously doubting she'd ever get the hang of what her aunt was trying to teach.

After carefully wrapping each amber dropper bottle in tissue and packing the remedies into a paper bag, Addie went to the register.

"Your remedies are ready whenever you are," she said.

Edna turned with a purse-lipped, sour expression. Heather's eyes were downcast, her gaze unfocused.

Edna tapped her daughter's arm. "Get my wallet?"

The younger woman reached into a backpack that was hooked over the back of Edna's seat and then rose and came to the counter. Edna shifted her scooter around to follow.

Addie rang up the tinctures and gave them the total.

With a hum of disapproval, Edna shook her head. "So much money for a bit of liquid in some glass."

Kate, who'd gone to clear the dishes from the table, caught Addie's eye. She had to swallow back a little laugh as Kate gave an exaggerated eyeroll.

Heather passed Addie some cash, she made change, and then the mother and daughter were on their way.

Pausing with the mugs and teapot in her hands, Kate watched them go.

"I would bet money Edna's not as sick as she makes out," she said.

Addie's brows lifted. "You think she's faking it?"

"At least a little. I always give people the benefit of the doubt, but if you ask me, I think she's exaggerating it all to keep Heather close. I've gotten an earful over the years about her various aches and pains, and none of those ailments should cause the level of helplessness she forces on her daughter."

"Huh," Addie said with surprise.

Aunt Kate wasn't the type of person to accuse someone else of lying without very good reason. She was trusting almost to a fault. If she thought Edna was exaggerating her condition, there was probably something to it.

Someone walked into the shop and called out Addie's name in a bright voice.

Addie grinned before she'd even turned around.

"Hey, Chelsea," she said as her friend walked in like a ray of sunshine with her blond hair in waves over her shoulders and the skirt of her yellow-and-white maxi dress swinging.

Chelsea said hello to Aunt Kate and came over to lean on the counter.

"I saw Heather and Edna leaving just now," Chelsea said. Her sunny expression turned sad. "Sometimes I wish I could just steal Heather away for a girls' night out or something. That poor woman never gets a break."

"I feel the same," Kate said from where she was standing at the apothecary shelves.

"So do you think Edna might not be as sick as she says, too?" Addie asked.

Chelsea's face turned wry, her mouth pressed into a line.

"I think she's really bitter and unhappy," she said. "And complaining and bossing her daughter around is basically all she's got in life."

Addie pulled her head back. "Yikes, that's a pretty sad existence."

"But if I'm right, it's at least partly her own making," Chelsea said with a shrug.

"Did you read her aura?" Addie asked, peering at her friend. "Is that why you think she's faking?"

"Maybe," Chelsea said with a little laugh. "But you don't always have to read auras to see what's going on, ya know?"

"Amen to that," Aunt Kate agreed.

"How are things going here?" Chelsea asked.

"Eh . . ." Addie said, shrugging. "I don't feel like I'm making much progress."

"Oh, that's not true," Kate said. "I keep telling her it takes time."

"Don't be too hard on yourself," Chelsea said.

Addie appreciated the support, but the truth was she still didn't know whether she really wanted to be able to put magic into remedies the way Aunt Kate used to. After so many years getting a science degree and then working in biotech, Addie was at home in the world of logic, research, and things that behaved in explainable ways. The things Kate was so patiently trying to teach were the exact opposite of all that.

Ever since learning Aunt Kate hadn't been murdered but had been saved from death by becoming a zombie—a Shuffler—Addie had felt torn. She wanted to help her aunt keep the shop open and would do almost anything to that end, but trying to channel magic? It was pushing Addie way beyond the boundaries of her comfort zone, and she really wished it wasn't necessary.

If she put her foot down and refused the magic part of Kate's training, her aunt might back off.

But the thing was, Addie had already experienced her own magic firsthand when she'd accidentally performed tasseomancy. She'd seen visions in tea leaves and heard voices speaking to her, and those things had helped catch the man who'd tried to kill Aunt Kate. Addie was grateful. But part of her also wished she could just go on with life and never think of that strange episode again.

Addie knew there was some sort of magic already in her. The tea-leaf reading had shown that. But that didn't mean she had to nurture it or even pay any attention to it.

"If it's okay, could Addie run to the bookstore with me really quick?" Chelsea asked.

"Sure, go, stretch your legs a little," Kate said, making shooing motions at them.

But Addie caught the strain on Kate's face and suppressed a sigh. Kate needed to get back to Shuffleville where she could be herself . . . whatever that meant these days.

"We should hurry," Addie said once they were outside. "Kate's tired, and I don't want to leave her alone for long."

Chelsea nodded, and they walked quickly past the yet-to-open guitar shop owned by Trey Parkinson, who'd come to Addie's rescue more than once.

Trey was inside sanding a piece of furniture. He gave Addie a broad smile, his green eyes sparkling, and she waved back. Trey was attractive in a rough-around-the-edges sort of way, and more than that, he seemed like a genuinely kind, good person. There'd been some subtle chemistry between them, but Addie hadn't acted on it because . . . well, for one thing she was fresh off a broken engagement to Dirtbag Jeremy whom she'd caught cheating.

But also, there was Bennett Brooks.

Yep, Bennett Brooks. Handsome with dark eyes, chestnut skin, and a penetrating gaze. Private and guarded. Mysterious, even.

Mmm-hmm, Bennett Brooks. And that was all Addie was going to allow herself to think about for the moment as far as men went.

At Enchanted Pages, Addie reached for the door just as someone else pushed it outward. She jumped back out of the way and started to apologize when she realized who it was.

Lisette Dubois Kumar.

"*Excuse* me," Lisette said, throwing up her hands as if Addie had been about to punch her.

The behavior wasn't surprising. Addie and Lisette had butted heads very recently, with Lisette accusing Kate of trying to steal business from the French café that Lisette and her husband owned. For a brief time, Addie had suspected that Lisette was the one who'd attacked Kate in her shop. That wasn't the case, but there was definitely some bad blood between them. And to add a layer of complication, Lisette had been Chelsea's nemesis when the two of them had been growing up in Stargaze.

Another woman followed Lisette. She was maybe ten years older than Addie's twenty-six years, her tank top showing her slim, toned arms, and her purple-streaked short hair artfully arranged with bangs sweeping her forehead to emphasize her large, amber-brown eyes.

The woman gave Addie a smile that somehow felt aggressive rather than friendly.

"I don't think we've met," the woman said to Addie.

Resisting the urge to step back from the woman, who'd moved forward and stuck out her hand, Addie straightened and stood her ground.

"I'm Yuna Akido," she said, giving Addie a significant look.

The woman acted as if she expected some kind of reaction on Addie's part, but she had no idea who this woman was. Her blank expression seemed to irritate Yuna, whose smile hardened.

"Addie James." She grasped Yuna's hand.

"Kate's niece," Yuna said, and Addie got the distinct sense that the slightly menacing woman had already known who Addie was.

"Yes," Addie said. "Nice to meet you."

Lisette was huffing and watching impatiently, so Addie pointed to the bookstore.

"Sorry, we're in a bit of a rush," she said. "We're just out for a quick errand."

"Oh, of course," Yuna said, finally moving away from the door so Addie and Chelsea could get past. "Have a nice afternoon."

After escaping inside, Addie turned to Chelsea.

"That was weird," Addie whispered.

"She's the mayor's wife," Chelsea whispered back. "She's a little full of herself."

"And she's friends with Lisette," Addie said, her mouth pinching.

"Yeah, that too," Chelsea said. "I'll be quick. I'm just grabbing a new journal from the gift area."

Addie lingered by the door rather than walking deeper into the store. The run-in with Lisette and Yuna had been unsettling, and Addie was also anxious to get back to Aunt Kate.

Chelsea completed her purchase, and the two of them headed back to Wild Rose Teas and Apothecary.

Kate was leaning over the counter, her eyes hollow and already bloodshot again.

"I'm sorry," she said. "But I need to get back to west Stargaze."

"Did you call Hank?" Addie asked.

Kate nodded. "He'll be here any minute."

Hank was also a Shuffler. He'd turned Aunt Kate into a zombie when he'd discovered her nearly dead after an attack. He'd saved her. If not for his actions, Kate would have died for real. Kate hadn't said it outright, but Addie suspected there might be something more than friendship between Hank and her aunt.

A few minutes later, Hank arrived in his pickup truck to whisk Kate away. Chelsea had to leave to get back to her clothing boutique, leaving Addie alone in the shop.

Addie had hoped the next hour before closing would pass uneventfully, but when the door opened and she saw Yuna coming in, Addie's stomach tightened.

She suddenly had the distinct feeling she wasn't going to end the shift so easily. And if she'd known what was coming, she would have shoved Yuna out the door and locked it.

Chapter Two

ADDIE FORCED A POLITE SMILE as Yuna Akido strode to the counter.

"Hello again," Addie said in her best customer-service voice. "How can I help you?"

Waiting on customers all day was almost the opposite of the type of work she was used to. Addie had moved to Stargaze after getting downsized from the San Francisco biotech company she'd worked for. She was used to spending her days in the lab, absorbing herself in experiments, and then sitting at her computer to crunch and analyze her experiment data. She was used to talking science and numbers with her co-workers, not listening to people's ailments and trying to come up with herbal remedies to ease their discomforts.

Smiling and being polite and helpful weren't exactly in her wheelhouse, but for Kate's sake Addie was doing her best. And she had to admit there was a certain satisfaction in helping people feel better that was very different than making a breakthrough in the lab.

Yuna's gaze skirted around the shop, and a vertical line formed between her brows as her face pulled down in a slight frown.

"Is Kate in the back?" she asked.

Addie shook her head and groaned internally. Some of Kate's regular clients were very put out when they would come in to find the regular proprietor wasn't there. Kate had built up trust with them over the years, so it was understandable that people didn't react the same way to Addie. But trying to help people who didn't really want to be dealing with her got a little tiresome.

"I'm closing up today, but I'd be glad to assist you," Addie said. "If you're coming for a refill of a remedy, I can look it up in Kate's records."

For a moment, Addie was sure Yuna was going to decline and leave. But then she gave a little sigh.

"Okay," Yuna said. "I've got the empty bottle, if you want to reuse it. I'll pay the full price, though. I don't need discounts."

Aunt Kate always offered her customers a bit of a price break if they recycled their bottles, but apparently Yuna was above pinching pennies.

She reached into her stylish white leather purse, a designer bag that had probably cost several hundred dollars, and produced a four-ounce amber dropper bottle.

As Yuna passed the bottle across the counter, her eyes narrowed slightly, and she seemed to quickly take in every detail of the shop, even twisting to look at the small café tables.

Just as Yuna's attention turned back to Addie, there was a soft jingling of a dog's collar on the stairs in the back.

Addie turned to see her little dog, Lucky, a stray who'd decided he belonged to her, coming down from the upstairs apartment that she'd taken over from Kate.

"Hey, little boy," Addie greeted Lucky with a smile. He wagged and came over to her, and she reached down and scratched behind his ears. "I'll take you out soon. Go lay down while I help this lady."

He peered up at Yuna for a moment but didn't seem interested in trying to make friends. Instead, he turned and went to the back corner where Addie had his bed set up.

"Excuse me," Addie said, setting down the bottle. "I'm going to wash my hands, and then I'll make up your tincture."

She went to the utility sink and then came back to the apothecary shelves and began pulling out bottles and setting them on what Kate referred to as the "mixing counter." Addie didn't need Kate's customer notebook after all because the bottle Yuna supplied had the ingredients and their proportions listed.

From what Addie had learned about herbs, the tincture appeared to be a formula for supporting a woman's hormones.

She pulled down thirty-two-ounce dark-brown bottles of Chaste Tree, Dandelion, Cramp Bark, and three Chinese herbs.

After some quick calculations using her phone's calculator and a scratch pad for jotting notes, she figured out the amounts needed from each bottle and poured them into a tiny glass cylinder with gradations marked on it, similar to the glassware she used to use in the lab.

The formula went into Yuna's bottle, and Addie screwed on the lid and gave it a gentle shake. All the while, she tried to drum up that magical *something* Aunt Kate had always put into her formulas. But Addie didn't feel any tingling or zips of energy or anything else Kate had mentioned as proof that the magic was working.

Yuna stashed the bottle in her purse, paid, and left.

Addie turned to her dog.

"Okay, Lucky, let's go take a spin around the neighborhood," she said. "I'll clean up for the day after we get back."

He jumped from his bed and trotted over to her. She grabbed the leash that was stashed under the counter, knowing she probably wouldn't end up using it. She'd learned Lucky wasn't the kind of dog to dart out into traffic or dash off chasing a squirrel.

Lucky didn't seem to be an ordinary dog in other ways, too. He seemed to understand everything Addie said to him, and even . . . well, it sounded ridiculous even admitting it in her head, but sometimes she almost suspected he could also hear and understand her thoughts.

Before they set out, Addie pulled out her phone and after a second of hesitation sent a text to Bennett:

I'm taking Lucky out for a short walk. We can swing by and get you if you'd like a break.

Bennett's office was only a couple of blocks away, and if he hadn't already gone home for the evening, maybe he'd be up for a stroll. Addie hadn't seen him much in the past couple of weeks. He'd been the one to finally tell her about the Shufflers and had in fact saved her from a horde of hungry zombies when she'd unknowingly gone into west Stargaze where the zombie community lived.

There was no reply to her message, and Addie tried not to feel disappointed. She decided they'd take the long way around the block, first heading in the opposite direction from Bennett's office so their walk wouldn't end too soon in case he wanted to join them.

She held the door for Lucky and then locked up Wild Rose Teas and Apothecary. With her phone stashed in the back pocket of her jeans, the store keys in one hand, and the folded leash in the other, she went past Trey's shop and then past the bookstore.

They made a circuit of the next block, coming back to pass Hair Affair, where Renaldo Hernandez was out front watering the petunias he and his sister Octavia had planted in brightly colored ceramic pots outside their salon.

"Hi, Addie," he said, giving her a little wave.

"Hi there," she said. She grasped the end of her ponytail as she passed. "I need to give you a call for a trim."

"Sounds good," he said with a nod.

Renaldo had shared a secret with her, one that she'd sworn to keep. He was in a romantic relationship with Adrian O'Conner, the owner of Enchanted Pages, but Renaldo's parents, who owned a nearby restaurant, didn't know he was gay. Addie hoped at some point he'd be able to talk to his family and not feel like he had to hide his true self or the person he loved. But she also knew Renaldo would have to do it in his own time and on his own terms.

At a storefront with a neon sign of a hand with a third-eye symbol in the palm, the door popped open and a woman with a high bun, bright-blue eyeshadow, and a purple and green Hawaiian print muumuu leaned out.

"Addie!" she waved. "I have something for you."

"Betty, how are you?"

"Fabulous, dearie, fabulous," the palm reader and astrologer said. "I've got a client in five minutes, though, so I can't chat."

She held out a book. Addie took it and read the cover.

Tasseomancy: The Art of Reading Tea Leaves

"Uh, thank you," Addie said. She tried to put on a gracious expression, but a book on tasseomancy wasn't exactly high on her reading list.

"Give it a read, and then Betty can answer any questions you have," Betty said, slipping into referring to herself in third person as she often did.

Then she disappeared back inside her "emporium," as she called it.

At the end of the block was Lisette's café, La Petite Patisserie. Addie loved Lisette's pastries as much as she disliked their baker.

A miniature crème brulee sure would hit the spot for dessert that night, though. Her mouth watered a little at the thought.

Addie slowed, trying to decide whether she wanted to go in and possibly have to deal with Lisette.

"You know what, Lucky?" Addie said quietly. "I'm not going to let her intimidate me. I'm a paying customer. She should be grateful for my patronage."

She clipped the leash onto Lucky's collar and tied the leash to the ornate iron bench outside the café. He hopped up and sat on the bench as if it were put there just for him. She wasn't really worried about him running off; the leash was mostly for show because people tended to get alarmed about an unleashed, unsupervised dog sitting on a bench.

Squaring her shoulders, she went inside. Several tables were occupied with early evening diners perusing menus. Lisette was extremely driven when it came to her café, and she'd recently decided to open for dinner. The café opened early, serving coffee drinks and pastries, and had always served lunch as well. Addie couldn't imagine the kind of hours Lisette and her husband, Raj, were putting in with the extended service. And dinners were more labor intensive and involved than coffee, pastries, or lunch.

She went up to the counter, where Raj was cleaning one of the espresso machines.

"What can I get for you?" he asked, offering her a polite smile.

Addie couldn't help sneaking a gaze toward the back.

"She's not here," Raj said in a low voice.

"Is it bad that I'm relieved?" Addie said with a soft laugh.

"I won't tell," he said with an amused look.

Lisette had a temper, and it turned out it didn't just manifest as rudeness and anger and hand-waving. When she really got worked up, it overflowed into something . . . supernatural. And sometimes a bit violent.

Addie had never seen it firsthand, but Chelsea had described an incident from when she and Lisette were teenagers where she'd gone into a jealous rage and telekinetically thrown some folding chairs at Chelsea. Addie might have been justified in doubting the story, except Raj had confirmed Lisette's ability to do such a thing.

Having paid for the crème brulee, Addie left the café with a white cardboard carton in her hand. Outside, she untied Lucky and then cast a look down the street at the building where Bennett's office was located. She checked her phone. Still no response.

"Oh well," she sighed.

She and Lucky crossed the street, passing Zelda's A to Z Antiques, and then came to Wild Rose, where she unlocked the door.

In the shop, she closed out the register, tidied the counter, and ran the vacuum over the floor. With the shop lights out and the sign turned to Closed, she and Lucky went up to the apartment.

Addie heated up a piece of leftover pizza for dinner, made a small side salad, and scooped some kibble into Lucky's bowl.

After finishing dinner and savoring every bite of the crème brulee, which had the most impossibly delicate toasted sugar crust on top that cracked so satisfyingly under her spoon, she cleaned up her dishes, showered, and fell into bed.

The next morning, she had a message from Kate, who said she was sorry but she wouldn't be able to make it into Wild Rose that day. She didn't offer an explanation, but Addie assumed it had something to do with how strained her aunt had looked the previous day.

Trying not to feel too disappointed, Addie took her cup of coffee and toast with jam down to start the store-opening procedure Kate had taught her.

When Addie went to unlock the front, she startled when she found someone suddenly standing on the other side of the glass door.

It was Yuna. She was dressed in a navy, fitted pants suit that showed off her trim, athletic figure, and she was carrying a tablet.

Addie opened the door.

"Hello, I'm here for the inspection," Yuna said in a businesslike voice.

Addie's mouth fell open in confusion. "Inspection? What are you inspecting?"

Yuna's manicured brows lifted sightly. "Oh, weren't you informed? I'm an Environmental Health Inspector with the local department. Please move aside so I can come in and begin."

With a sinking stomach, Addie stepped out of the way.

Yuna came in, scanned Wild Rose with a look on her face as if she were a cat ready to bite the head off an unsuspecting mouse, and powered up her tablet.

Chapter Three

FEELING A STRANGE MIX OF dread and confusion, Addie watched Yuna Akido work on her tablet for a few seconds.

"Uh, what are you going to be looking at?" Addie asked, finally finding her voice.

"Everything that could impact the health of your customers," Yuna said.

"But Wild Rose isn't a restaurant," Addie said. "Aren't these inspections only for restaurants?"

Yuna spared a quick glance up from her tablet, and the look on her face was one of both authority and satisfaction. She was clearly enjoying the fact that she'd caught Addie off guard.

"No, they're not just for restaurants," Yuna said. "But seeing as how Kate has elected to serve beverages made in-store and"—she tapped her tablet stylus on the empty pastry case on the counter—"non-packaged food items, this establishment now warrants a full inspection."

Addie had no idea if this was true. She didn't know anything about health inspections or qualifying as a restaurant. Turning away, she pulled out her phone and dialed Aunt Kate.

Please pick up. Please, please pick up.

But the call went to voicemail. Addie left a message in an urgent whisper, asking Kate to call back right away.

Just as she was disconnecting, Lucky appeared on the stairs. Addie's eyes popped wide.

Oh no.

A dog wandering free in a restaurant? That was certainly going to be some kind of major violation.

Addie hurried to intercept Lucky and herd him back up the stairs, where she closed the apartment door to keep him out of sight. There was a soft plaintive whine and the sound of nails scratching at the door.

"Sorry, boy," she whispered and then went back down.

It was a pointless gesture to contain Lucky upstairs, most likely, because he had been down in the store the previous day when Yuna had come in for her remedy.

Aunt Kate had said nothing about inspections, and during all the summers Addie had spent with her aunt, she couldn't recall ever being at Wild Rose when a health inspector had been there. Maybe this was a new thing since Kate had added the little café tables and, as Yuna had pointed out, the pastry case on the counter.

Regardless, Kate would know what to do. Addie stared at her phone, willing it to ring, but it stayed stubbornly silent. She thumbed a text message that reiterated her voicemail: *S.O.S.*

And then she watched helplessly as Yuna walked around the shop tapping and writing on her tablet with the stylus. She asked questions here and there, which Addie answered the best she could.

When Yuna was busy in the back, Addie sent another urgent message, this one to Chelsea. Her store was a clothing boutique and wasn't subject to restaurant health inspections, but Addie couldn't think of who else to ask for help.

Suddenly having the sense of eyes on her, Addie looked out the window.

Across the street to the left, a figure stood in the front window of La Petite Patisserie.

It was Lisette, and even from that distance, Addie could see the cold, satisfied smile on the café owner's red-lipsticked lips.

Addie's eyes narrowed, and anger flashed hotly through her chest.

Had Lisette somehow put Yuna up to this? That was certainly the vibe Addie was getting from across the street.

Grinding her teeth, Addie tried to ignore Yuna and finish the morning checklist for opening the shop. There would be customers, and Addie wasn't going to let Yuna throw off the day any more than she already had.

At least, that was what Addie told herself.

But by the time the inspector left, Addie felt like a cold, hard knot had taken up residence in the spot where her stomach should be.

Her phone rang. It was Chelsea.

"Please tell me Wild Rose isn't going to get shut down," Addie said by way of greeting.

"Take a breath, hon," Chelsea said in a soothing voice. "You're not going to get shut down."

"Are you sure?"

"Well, I guess I can't say I'm positive, but I can't imagine there are any violations in the shop that are that serious."

Addie puffed her cheeks and blew out a slow stream of air, trying to calm down.

"Wild Rose is Kate's life's work," Chelsea continued. "She wouldn't have knowingly done anything to jeopardize it."

"You're right on the one hand," Addie said. "But she can be pretty absentminded even when she has the best intentions. And with what happened to her recently, well, I wouldn't blame her if some important things slipped her mind." She distractedly ran her hand over her hair, pushing stray strands behind her ear. "I tried to call her, and I sent a text, but I haven't heard back."

"I'm sure she'll be in touch soon," Chelsea said. "And in the meantime, you could go talk the Hernandezes. They have literally years of experience with this sort of thing."

Javier's was a Mexican Restaurant owned and run by the Hernandez family, minus Renaldo and Octavia, who'd split from the family business to start their hair salon. Addie had been enjoying the amazing food at Javier's since she was a kid visiting Aunt Kate during summer breaks.

"Oh, that's a good idea," Addie said. She leaned a hip against the counter. "You know, I get the feeling Lisette might be behind this inspection."

"Really?"

"Yeah. I saw her staring through the window while Yuna was here. Lisette had a very self-satisfied Cheshire grin on her face."

"That would be an ugly thing for her to do," Chelsea said.

"Well, she was really upset about Kate putting in wi-fi and tables and serving drinks and pastries, remember?"

"Shoot, that's right. How could I have forgotten that?"

"I wouldn't mind calling her out on it, if it's true," Addie said.

"Why don't we have dinner at the café tonight?" Chelsea suggested. "The Patisserie is still trying to get off the ground with their dinner service, so Lisette waits tables."

"Yes," Addie said nodding. "We'll make sure to sit in her section. She can't be openly rude to us in front of other customers, and she'll have to control her . . . *temper*. Because if there's one thing she wants in life, it's for that place to be a raging success. She wouldn't risk that by blowing up at paying customers in public."

"Exactly," Chelsea said. "I'll come to Wild Rose right before you close, and we can walk over there. In fact, I'm going to call right now and make a reservation, and I'll make sure to request Lisette as our server."

"Thank you, Chels. See you this evening."

Addie felt a little better after hanging up. If Lisette had prodded Yuna to target Wild Rose, it might be hard to prove, but at least Addie wouldn't just be standing by and letting Lisette bully her.

Business was steady for the rest of the day, and without Kate there to give Addie a break, Addie didn't get the chance to talk to Javier Hernandez about how to handle inspections.

All she had time to do was take Lucky outside for a quick jaunt down the block to relieve himself. She felt bad keeping him cooped up in the apartment. He was so well-behaved in the store. He never bothered the rare customer who wasn't a dog person, and he delighted in those who were.

Before she knew it, the workday was nearly over.

She quickly ran through the closing checklist and was just finishing the register close-out when Chelsea walked in dressed in a flowy multicolored boho skirt, a white halter top that showed a strip of tanned stomach, and an armful of gold bangles that tinkled cheerily.

"Hi," Addie called, giving her friend a bright smile. "Could you flip the sign over for me?"

"Sure." Chelsea doubled back to turn the sign to Closed.

"I'm going to change clothes really fast, and then we can go," Addie said, and then she turned and took the stairs two at a time up to the apartment.

There, she threw on a cute A-line skirt with a black-and-white chevron pattern paired with a sky-blue tank top in a chunky sweater knit. She didn't want to take the time to refresh her makeup, but she pulled her long hair back into a sleek ponytail and slipped on a black velvet headband. White kitten heel mules completed the outfit.

She poured some food for Lucky, gave him fresh water, and then bent to scratch him under the chin.

"I promise we'll go for a W-A-L-K and hang out later," she said.

He started wagging his tail and hopping back and forth, letting out a couple of excited little yips.

"Don't tell me you know how to spell now," Addie said, straightening, placing her hands on her hips, and smiling down at him. "You're such a good boy. I don't care what that stupid health inspector puts in her report. I'll be back soon."

She grabbed her purse, blew him a kiss at the door, and then closed it.

Downstairs, Chelsea was looking at her phone.

"I texted Pete to see if he'd heard anything through the grapevine about inspections," she said.

They walked together to the door and out to the sidewalk, where Addie locked the shop and slipped the keys into her purse.

"He's the guy at Grinning Catfish Brewery, right? Maybe he'll know something." Addie said. "Although I don't think Lisette has a vendetta against *him*."

At the end of the block, they crossed over to La Petite Patisserie, which was located on the opposite corner.

Inside, Chelsea stepped up to the hostess at the podium and gave her the reservation info.

Addie peered around and spotted Lisette waiting on a table near the window to the right. Their eyes met, and Lisette's face hardened before she looked down at the small notepad she was writing on.

The hostess seated Addie and Chelsea at a table near the door.

The place was gorgeous, Addie grudgingly admitted silently, with its French farmhouse décor. Beautiful glass chandeliers, quaint wood chairs, white painted pedestal tables, a whitewashed wood accent wall, a long butcherblock counter that displayed the old-fashioned register, and gleaming copper cookware hanging over the pastry cases.

Lisette had great taste and a keen eye; there was no denying it. She'd added white linens for dinner, and candles on each table sat in an eclectic array of antique glasses.

The place was busy, too.

"Big crowd tonight," Addie said as she opened the menu.

"Yeah, I saw that Lisette put an ad in the newspaper and posted on several of the Stargaze neighborhood forums," Chelsea said. "It seems to have done the trick."

Addie was facing the door, and when a couple walked in, she couldn't help stiffening.

"Oh great, Yuna's here," she murmured.

Chelsea glanced over her shoulder as Yuna, dressed in a form-fitting aqua dress and black heels, was speaking to the hostess. The man who was with her also appeared quite fit, with a trim waist and muscled biceps just showing below the short sleeves of his crisp white button-down.

"That's Mayor Akido," Chelsea said.

The pair made a striking couple—confident, attractive, and athletic.

The mayor had a small gym bag in hand, which he pushed under his chair when he sat. His hair was damp, and his cheeks were slightly flushed. Addie guessed he'd come straight from a workout.

"Would you like to order drinks while you're deciding?"

Addie jumped and turned to Lisette, who'd appeared by the table as Addie had been busy watching the mayor and his wife. Lisette glared at Addie and then at Chelsea as if they were being a terrible inconvenience.

Addie frowned. Lisette could at least pretend to be polite.

"A glass of the chardonnay for me," Addie said.

Chelsea straightened in her chair. "Same, please. But before you go, we'd like to ask you about something." She gave Addie a look.

Addie swallowed. "Yes. That's right."

"Well, can you spit it out? You might have noticed we're at capacity. I don't have time for chitchat," Lisette said.

Wow. She wasn't even pretending to be polite.

"Are you trying to get Yuna to put Wild Rose out of business?" Addie asked.

Might as well get to the point. That was what Lisette wanted, after all.

"Excuse me?" Lisette pulled her head back with a haughty look.

"That's not an answer," said Chelsea.

"No, I'm not," the café owner said, biting off the words. "I'll be back with your wine."

She turned on her heel and stalked over to the end of the counter.

"Maybe this was a mistake," Addie said. "It sounded like a good idea earlier, but now, it seems a little fruitless. Even if we're right, she's not going to admit it."

"But at least she knows we're onto her," Chelsea said. "Plus, I kind of like that she has to wait on us."

That got a small smile from Addie.

Lisette returned with the wine, and she took their orders. Chicken confit for Chelsea, and quiche lorraine for Addie.

Addie picked up her wine glass and looked around at the full restaurant. Only a booth and a small table were empty.

"Good thing you made a reservation," she said.

"Hey, even if our mission is a bust, we know the food is going to be divine," Chelsea said.

She held out her glass. They clinked and then sipped. The chardonnay was delicate and had the ideal balance of acidity, sweetness, and dryness. A perfect glass on a late summer evening.

Addie was just starting to think she might actually enjoy the dinner when a sudden movement at the mayor's table caught her eye.

Yuna was sitting with her back to Addie. The woman's shoulders jerked. Then she stood so abruptly her chair toppled backward.

"What the—" Chelsea twisted around.

Addie hurriedly set her glass down as Yuna took one staggering step. The mayor jumped up and moved toward her. One of her ankles buckled, and her leg folded under her.

Yuna reached for the table to catch herself but caught only a handful of tablecloth. Her glass of red wine fell, the glass shattering on the floor and splashing red liquid over her husband's khaki pants.

The mayor reached out, but only caught her wrist as Yuna collapsed to the floor.

Alarmed exclamations filled the café, and Addie ran over to Yuna.

"Is she choking?" Addie asked.

"No, she hasn't eaten anything yet," the mayor said. He bent over her. "Yuna? Yuna!"

The woman was unresponsive, her face slack and her lids closed. A woman in black slacks and a fluttery lavender shirt elbowed in. "I'm an EMT," she said.

She pushed her thick blond hair over her shoulder and bent over Yuna.

"Does she have any allergies?" the EMT asked.

"No, no, nothing," the mayor said.

His face was oddly blank. He must have been in shock.

"She's not breathing," the EMT muttered and then called out, "We need an ambulance!"

"It's on the way," someone said.

Addie looked up to see it was Lisette's husband, Raj, who was holding his phone. He'd been the one to speak.

Lisette had run up beside him from the back, and when she took in the scene, she slapped her hand over her mouth and let out a sharp scream behind her hand. Her eyes were wide and round.

The EMT pushed Yuna over onto her back and into rescue-breathing position and began the procedure. When the EMT paused to take a pulse, her face went from tense to grim. She started chest compressions.

Addie gasped. Yuna not only wasn't breathing, but her heart must have stopped, too.

The mayor was on his knees next to his wife with his hands propped on his thighs, watching her with unblinking eyes. He seemed almost detached from what was happening in front of him.

The next several minutes were a blur as the EMT continued CPR until the ambulance arrived. Yuna was swiftly loaded onto a stretcher and whisked away with her husband riding in the back and the siren wailing.

All of the diners had left their tables, and some had moved outside to watch the ambulance depart. Everyone was visibly shaken.

Chelsea hooked her arm through Addie's, and they gave each other a long look.

The EMT was standing right next to them, pushing her hair back from her flushed, sweaty face. Another woman, a brunette the EMT had been dining with, was trying to console her.

"You did all you could," the brunette woman said, placing a hand on the EMT's shoulder.

"It's no use," the EMT said. "There was no pulse. I think she was dead when she hit the floor."

Addie inhaled sharply through her nose.

She stared at the chair where Yuna had been sitting only moments earlier.

And it was then that Addie noticed the wine glass wasn't the only thing that had fallen and shattered. On the floor was the amber dropper bottle with a Wild Rose Teas and Apothecary label on it—the very one Addie had filled for Yuna the evening before. The neck of the bottle had snapped off when it hit the floor, spilling dark liquid that mingled with the red wine.

Addie's blood went cold as she realized she was looking at the scene of a death, and something she'd made was right in the middle of it.

Chapter Four

ADDIE WAS FROZEN ON THE spot, staring at the broken
apothecary bottle.

The bottle had fallen to the floor most likely because Yuna had
pulled it out and taken some of the tincture. Her purse was still
upright on the floor next to her chair, so if she hadn't been using
the tincture it would still be in her bag.

Had Yuna really taken some of the remedy right before she
collapsed?

Addie's heart began to pound as she wondered if she'd put an
incorrect herb into Yuna's formula. It was a remedy Yuna had used
before, so if Addie had re-made it correctly, it shouldn't have caused
the woman any trouble.

But could Addie have accidentally added something Yuna had
reacted to?

Addie strained to remember. It'd been the end of the day, and
she'd been tired. She'd also been slightly unnerved by Yuna's
less-than-friendly demeanor.

But Addie had years of experience mixing chemicals in the lab,
and she knew how to be careful.

"Hey, you're white as a sheet," Chelsea said, peering at Addie's face. "Maybe we should go back to Wild Rose."

Chelsea looked shaken, too, her eyes round and her lips parted as she shifted her gaze to once again take in the overturned chair, the tablecloth that had been pulled askew, and the mess on the floor.

For a second, Addie was going to agree, but it seemed wrong to just leave Yuna's purse on the floor.

She went to pick it up, intending to leave it with Lisette, but then spotted the mayor's gym bag peeking out from under his chair. Addie pulled it out.

It was open, and inside were three prescription bottles. She wasn't trying to get a look at them, but she noticed they all had "Westside Pharmacy" labels on them.

She happened to see two of the medication names, too, though they were long words she didn't recognize right off.

After zipping up the bag, she lifted it in one hand and grabbed Yuna's purse in the other. Lisette was standing nearby, her face against Raj's shoulder as her shoulders trembled.

Addie caught Raj's eye and went up to him.

"I thought you might want to hold onto these for Mayor Akido," Addie said.

"Sure," Raj said, his dar-brown eyes solemn. "If you could leave them under the register, we'll take care of them."

Lisette didn't acknowledge Addie.

She dropped the two bags on a shelf under the counter and then went back to Chelsea.

Addie's fingers itched with the urge to pick up the apothecary bottle. Knowing it was just sitting there for anyone to see made her jumpy.

"Want to go?" Chelsea asked.

Addie nodded, but she didn't move.

Chelsea frowned. "What is it?"

Addie lifted her chin, indicating the bottle on the floor. "I made that remedy for Yuna yesterday," she whispered. "I think . . . I think she might have used it right before she—she . . ." Unable to finish the sentence, she looked helplessly at Chelsea.

"Oh," Chelsea said, her blond brows rising.

They both stared at the bottle for a moment. Addie was just about to reach for a napkin from the table next to her so she could use it to push the broken glass into a pile—and take the opportunity to stash the apothecary bottle in the pocket of her skirt—when a police car rolled to a stop at the curb, its bubble lights on but no siren.

Addie pulled her hand back guiltily.

Officer Davis, whom Addie had dealt with when Aunt Kate had been attacked, unfolded his tall frame and got out from behind the wheel of the cruiser.

He'd been nice to Addie before, for the most part, but right then she had absolutely no desire to be talking to a police officer about what had just happened.

"If I could get everyone to stick around long enough for me to take down your name, I'd really appreciate it," he called out.

"Why do you need our names?" asked the blond EMT. "The mayor's wife likely had some kind of allergic reaction or cardiac event. It's not like someone here caused what happened."

Addie swallowed hard.

"Just the same, if anything comes up, I'd like to know who witnessed this unfortunate event," Officer Davis said.

He stood in the doorway with a small notebook and pen, and people started to form a loose line to get out. Everyone stayed well clear of the table where the Akidos had been.

Addie cast another look at the bottle on the floor. She couldn't very well pick it up now. Someone would definitely see, and it would look suspicious.

She and Chelsea waited in line. Before they got to the doorway, a sedan pulled up behind the cruiser. An unsmiling woman with curly red hair dressed in a dark suit got out.

Detective Julia McCann. Not Addie's favorite person.

Her insides clenched as she gave Officer Davis her name and stepped out onto the sidewalk just as the detective was coming up to the café's door.

Chelsea and Addie escaped to Wild Rose and went upstairs to the apartment, where Addie heated up some soup that neither of them really wanted to eat and set a box of crackers on the coffee table while the two of them sat on the sofa.

"What if she reacted to my tincture, Chels?" Addie asked in a small voice. "It was a refill, but maybe I made it incorrectly."

"You didn't," Chelsea said firmly. "This didn't happen because of you."

Addie slumped. "I just can't help thinking I might have done something wrong."

Lucky came and rested his chin on the sofa next to her knee, and she reached out to pet his head.

"It's going to be okay," Chelsea promised.

Addie nodded and forced a tiny smile, but it was mostly in an effort to make Chelsea feel better.

"It's getting late," Addie said. "I should let you get home."

They rose, and Chelsea gave Addie a hug that smelled like a summer evening—jasmine, vanilla, and orange with a slight undertone of frankincense. It was a warm, cheerful, and comforting scent.

Addie and Lucky walked Chelsea to her car, a pale-yellow VW Bug convertible that was somehow the exact automobile embodiment of Chelsea's personality.

Then Addie took Lucky around the block. When Bennett's office came into view, Addie looked to see if there was a light in the window. Not having a family to go home to, sometimes he was there late. But that night, the windows were dark.

Feeling forlorn and out of sorts, Addie went back to her apartment where she quickly showered and got ready for bed.

It took a good hour of staring at the ceiling and worrying before she finally drifted off to sleep.

The next day was Sunday, and Addie and Kate had decided to reduce the store hours to ten to two on Sundays during the less busy seasons. It was late summer, and tourist traffic had slowed considerably. That meant Addie could sleep in.

But at eight in the morning on the dot, there was an insistent knocking on the shop door. It was loud enough to rouse Lucky, who jumped up on Addie.

She got out of bed, threw on a bathrobe, and irritably stalked down the stairs.

When she saw Detective McCann on the other side of the glass door, Addie stopped short.

A weekend visit from the detective? It had to be related to Yuna's death. Addie's stomach started a slow churn as she went to let Detective McCann in.

"Sorry to have woken you," Julia McCann said, taking in Addie's bathrobe and hair, which was likely a mess after she'd gone to bed with a wet head following her shower.

"What can I do for you?" Addie asked, closing the door and then crossing her arms tightly over her robe.

"I'm here concerning the incident at the Patisserie last night."

"Is it true?" Addie asked. "Is Yuna really dead?"

"Unfortunately, yes."

Addie shook her head slowly, trying not to think about the broken apothecary bottle. "Her poor husband. He was right there. It happened before his eyes."

"What was your relationship to the deceased?" McCann asked, pulling out her notebook and pen.

"We didn't have one. I only just met her two days ago," Addie said.

"Were you here when she came to purchase a remedy that day?"

Addie's heart dropped, and then her pulse began to thump fast and hard.

"Uh, yes," Addie said reluctantly.

"And what about your aunt? Was she here as well?"

"No, it was just me."

Detective McCann looked up from her notebook, her face unreadable and her blue eyes sharp on Addie.

"And during Mrs. Akido's visit here, you made an herbal concoction for her?" the detective asked.

"A tincture. Yes, I did."

"What was in it?"

Addie rattled off the list of ingredients from memory. "It was a refill of a tincture she'd used several times before."

"What's the purpose of the tincture?"

"I didn't create it originally," Addie said. "The discussion about Yuna's needs was with my aunt, not me. I was merely duplicating the formula that Yuna had used before."

"But you must know, even in a general sense, what the various ingredients were for."

For a moment, Addie didn't respond. "I'm sorry, but I don't feel comfortable discussing that. It feels like a violation of Yuna's privacy."

McCann flipped back a couple of pages in her notebook.

"From what I found on Google, the herbs on the label of the bottle are mostly for hormone-related complaints. Does that sound right?"

Addie pressed her mouth into a tense line. They'd found the bottle on the floor, obviously. The detective had already done her research on the herbs, but she was probably going to try to get Addie to do more than just confirm what Google had already said.

"In general, that sounds right," Addie said finally.

"And why would she need a hormonal remedy?"

"That I don't know. She just wanted a refill. She didn't discuss any specifics with me."

"Hmm," the detective murmured as she wrote a few notes.

"Why are you asking about the remedy?"

The detective gave Addie another sharp look. "We're exploring all avenues in this case."

"Case?" Addie frowned. "That sounds like you suspect foul play."

"I didn't say that," the detective said. "It's our job to be thorough." She flipped her notebook closed. "Where is your aunt? Is she upstairs?"

Addie shook her head. "She's away."

"I need to speak with her, so please have her contact me at her earliest convenience." McCann passed a business card to Addie.

"Will do," Addie said.

"I'll be in touch with you again soon," the detective added. "And I'm going to be frank. You need to stay here in town for the time being."

Addie's mouth went dry.

"Why? Do you think I had something to do with Yuna's death?" she asked, her pulse bumping again.

"Like I said, we're exploring all possibilities."

Addie tried to probe again, but the detective refused to comment any further and made her exit.

Addie felt sick as she trudged back up to the apartment. Sitting huddled on the sofa, she began sending urgent messages to Kate, Bennett, and Chelsea, and it was all she could do to fight the panic that was threatening to take over.

Chapter Five

ADDIE WOODENLY WENT THROUGH THE motions of getting ready for the day and opening the shop.

Chelsea had called right away after Addie's text, promising to come over as soon as Wild Rose closed.

And to Addie's enormous relief, Kate finally responded. She sent a text saying she'd been in the throes of hunger—apparently she'd pushed herself too much and gone too long without eating—and after she finally ate, she went into a deep sleep for almost a full day.

Addie was trying to be understanding, not to mention doing her best to avoid thinking about exactly *what* Aunt Kate had been eating, but really needed help and support. Aunt Kate promised to come that afternoon, and that made Addie feel about twenty pounds lighter.

There was no reply from Bennett, and Addie wasn't sure she knew him and his habits well enough yet to be worried. She would ask Kate later. She and Bennett had been friends for some time, and she'd probably know if it was time to go knock on his door or make more of an effort to track him down.

Feeling relieved enough to focus on the store, Addie helped a dozen customers throughout the day. Some just wanted to buy tea, but a few came in for herbal remedies. She did her best to try to imbue healing intention into each tincture but doubted she was accomplishing anything magical. Still, she figured it couldn't hurt to toss out some positive thoughts toward the remedies and the people who needed them.

Finally, it was nearly time to close up for the day.

Addie was making a list of items that needed to be reordered when someone opened the door. She looked up, and her knees nearly buckled with relief at the sight of Aunt Kate.

"I'm so glad you're here," was all Addie could choke out.

She went to her aunt, who wrapped her in a tight hug.

"You've been through a lot," Kate said, pulling back to look at Addie. "Even without the detective's visit, seeing someone die is deeply traumatic."

Letting out a long breath, Addie nodded.

"I'm really worried about the detective, though," she said. "Oh, and by the way, she wants to talk to you. I've got her card here somewhere."

Kate scrunched her mouth to the side. "Well, I'm not in a huge hurry to make that call. Let me help you close up, and then we can talk some more."

As they were finishing the closing checklist, Chelsea showed up. She made a pot of peppermint tea and poured cups for the three of them. When Kate and Addie had finished their chores, they all sat down at one of the tables.

For a moment, they just relaxed and sipped their tea.

"Do you want to tell us what the detective said?" Chelsea suggested.

Addie recounted the entire exchange.

"She wouldn't say it was foul play, but it was pretty clear the police suspect Yuna didn't die of natural causes," she said.

"Well, I don't think we should jump to conclusions," Kate said, patting Addie's hand.

Aunt Kate's green pallor was hidden under tinted moisturizer, and the whites of her eyes were clear, in contrast to a couple of days before when they'd become alarmingly bloodshot. Her energy seemed to have returned, too.

A serving of—Addie winced internally—*human brains* had apparently been just what Kate needed. She and the rest of the Shufflers who lived in the zombie community in west Stargaze had people helping them gain access to human brains. It was the only sustenance Shufflers could eat, and they needed it to stay alive. Or maybe not *alive* alive, but whatever the zombie equivalent of alive was.

A sharp knock at the door made all three of them jump and swivel around to see who was there.

It was Detective McCann. Did the woman ever take a day off?

"Oh no," Addie groaned.

"I'll let her in," Kate said, rising and going to the door.

She exchanged a few words with the detective and then led her to where the three women had been sitting with their tea.

"Would you like a cup of peppermint?" Kate offered.

McCann held up her hand. "No, but thank you."

Addie saw Officer Davis pull up in his cruiser, but he stayed in the car.

"Is there news about Yuna?" Addie asked, hoping against hope that a coroner had determined Yuna died of a stroke or some other untimely but natural cause.

"Yes, in fact," the detective said. "The medical examiner believes her heart stopped because she was poisoned."

Addie's lips parted in shock. "What kind of poison?"

"Those tests are currently in progress," McCann said. She homed in on Addie. "The health inspection records show Mrs. Akido was here recently."

For a moment, Addie's mind blanked and she blinked a couple of times.

"She was. It was Friday. First thing in the morning," she said.

Kate made a soft noise, a quiet but sharp intake of breath. Her eyes widened slightly. But McCann didn't seem to notice.

"And what occurred during that inspection?" McCann asked.

"Uh, I guess she did what she normally does?" Addie said uncertainly. "I'd never been through one before. She walked around and looked at everything, asked me some questions, and made a lot of notes."

The detective's eyes narrowed. "And how did it go?"

Addie skirted a glance at Aunt Kate, who had definitely tensed since the topic of the inspection had come up.

"Well, not great, I guess," Addie said slowly. "She indicated there were probably going to be some violations."

"I see." McCann wrote in her notebook for a few seconds. "And were these going to be first-time violations?"

"I don't know," Addie said, shaking her head and looking at her aunt.

"Oh dear," Aunt Kate said. "It seems I failed to inform Addie about some issues. I've not been well lately and had to take quite a bit of time off. The last inspection slipped my mind. I was supposed to make some changes."

Was that true, or was Kate just trying to take some of the attention off Addie?

"Hmm, okay." The detective made more notes, and it appeared she felt what Kate just said was somehow significant. Then she closed her notebook. "Here's the thing. It appears that Yuna's recommendation after the most recent inspection was to close down this establishment until certain things could be brought up to code."

Addie frowned. "She didn't say that. She never said anything to indicate it was that serious.

McCann ignored Addie's comment and continued, "And again, to be frank, I'm not liking the connections I'm seeing here."

"What do you mean?" Kate asked.

"The woman who was ready to shut down your business just died suddenly of apparent poisoning," the detective said. "And just before she died, she took some of the liquid from the bottle Addie made up for her."

Was she really saying . . . ?

Dark dread began to fill Addie.

"But I made that remedy before she even did the inspection!" Addie burst out, her heart racing with near panic at what McCann was suggesting. "When I made her tincture, I didn't even know about the other inspection. Kate just said she'd forgotten about all that and never told me. I had no idea there were violations or that Wild Rose was in any peril. And anyway, there was nothing poisonous in the bottle! It was a remedy she'd used before. This is just . . . *crazy*. The order of events is wrong. You're grasping at straws."

"Only if you and your aunt are telling the truth," McCann said, her face hard as stone.

"So, what, are you going to arrest me?" Addie demanded.

"Oh, surely not. Let's all just take a breath," Kate soothed.

But it was too late. The detective seemed to already be drawing conclusions about Addie's involvement, and Addie was already too far into panic.

"We won't be making an arrest right now," McCann said to Addie. "But we're going to post an officer outside the shop while we await results of the tests to pinpoint the source of the poisoning. Stargaze Police is officially requesting that you do not leave the city limits."

"You're putting me under house arrest?" Addie asked incredulously.

"No, not yet," Detective McCann said.

Not *yet*?

"Detective McCann, it seems like you're targeting Addie without enough reason," Chelsea said in a warm tone and putting on a friendly face. "I've known her since we were children, and I would swear on my life she would never do what you're suggesting."

"Additional information has come out that I can't disclose at this time," the detective said. "All I can say is that it doesn't look good for Addie. I'll be in touch soon."

Chelsea's smile faltered.

This was a nightmare. That was it. Addie was still asleep, and this was all just a horrible, horrible dream.

In a daze, Addie sank to her chair and watched the detective leave.

"It makes no sense," she said weakly. "I didn't know about the inspection. I have no reason to hurt a woman I'd barely just met. I have no reason to hurt *anyone*."

She couldn't say anything more as a lump formed in her throat. With tears welling in her lower lids, she looked between Kate and Chelsea and saw two faces reflecting disbelief.

Chelsea gave her head a shake. "Nothing will come of this. When those results come back, they're going to be apologizing to you. Just you wait and see."

But Kate didn't jump in with reassurances.

"I'm so sorry, Addie," she said in a low voice. "I think this is all my fault. I forgot about the inspection and the list of infractions I needed to correct."

"Was it really that bad, though?" Addie asked in a wavering voice as she swiped the tears from under her eyes. "I figured Lucky being in here would be the worst violation. Yuna said this is now considered a restaurant because you serve tea and sometimes have scones and such. Having a dog in a restaurant had to be the biggest black mark against us."

Perhaps hearing his name, the little dog appeared at the bottom of the stairs and padded over to them. He jumped up on Addie's lap and sat there, leaning against her as if trying to offer comfort.

Kate let out a heavy sigh. "Remember how upset Lisette was? How she accused me of opening a competing café right across the street?"

"How could I forget," Addie said wryly.

"That seems so silly now," Chelsea said. "Back then, Lisette was basically running a coffee and pastry café. She only did a light lunch menu. Now that she's doing full sit-down dining for dinner, it seems even more ridiculous that she considered some tea, free internet, and donuts a threat."

"I agree," Kate said. "But nevertheless, it really pushed her buttons. She and Yuna were working to change the local code so that the definition of 'restaurant' became a whole lot more encompassing than it used to be."

"So, she wanted Wild Rose to get classified as a restaurant; then Yuna would come in here and write you up, and together they'd try to force you out of business," Addie said. "Or at the very least force you to go back to only selling tea and apothecary items. I *knew* Lisette was connected to all of this somehow."

"Did they succeed in changing the code?" Chelsea asked.

"Unfortunately, yes," Kate said grimly. "It happened right before I was attacked. I literally didn't remember it until the detective was talking. The change I went through affected my memory, and there are some pretty big gaps. I forgot my email password, too, and I bet there are a bunch of messages about all this. I should have been more on top of things. I shouldn't have put so much responsibility on you, Addie."

"You're doing your best," Addie said. "But wouldn't they have sent something official through the regular mail?"

"They probably did," Kate said with a rueful look toward the basket on the back counter where she always put the day's mail. "I probably opened it right before I was attacked. That's when all of this was coming to a head. I'll search through my files and also get back into my email account. I'll give you the password, too, so this won't happen again."

Addie tried not to feel frustrated with her aunt. Kate was one of the kindest people she knew, but she was a self-confessed scatterbrain, and the attack aside, this wasn't the first time her disorganization had caused problems for her.

Instead of focusing on impatience, Addie silently vowed to put some systems in place. It was the kind of thing her logic-loving mind was good at.

"As much as I hate to say it, I think we need to do something," Addie said reluctantly.

"Like what?" Chelsea asked.

"Try to figure out who might have poisoned Yuna."

Kate straightened. "We should get Bennett to help. I'm sure he'd be glad to."

"I've sent him a few messages in the past couple of days," Addie said with a shrug. "He hasn't answered."

"He might be on a stakeout," Kate said. "Sometimes people hire him to follow a spouse suspected of cheating, that sort of thing. It could be a job out of town. But I don't like that he isn't responding." She reached for her phone. "It looks like the police are keeping an eye on you, Addie, so you should stay here for now, I think. I'm going to call Hank and ask him to drive me to Bennett's house."

"You still don't feel up to driving?" Addie asked.

Kate shook her head. "The dizzy spells aren't as bad as they used to be, but I figure better safe than sorry." She rose and walked toward the counter to make her phone call.

Addie stared at a spot on the floor, feeling helpless. She was a suspect. Or the nearest thing to it.

Frowning, she suddenly recalled something that she'd paid little attention to at the time it'd happened.

"You know, there's something you could try," Chelsea said quietly as she poured more tea into Addie's cup. "Something you can do right here. It might really help your cause."

Addie looked up hopefully, sidetracked from the thought she'd had a few seconds before.

Chelsea lifted her own mug. "Tea leaves. You could try to do a reading."

"Oh no, not that," Addie groaned, remembering the book on tasseomancy Betty had given her.

Her friend gave a little shrug. "It helped last time."

"Yeah, it did. Maybe I'll try it later. But I just remembered something, and I think it's going to help us start our list of suspects in Yuna's poisoning."

"Really?" Chelsea reached into her bag and pulled out her journal and purple gel pen. "Do tell."

She uncapped her pen and looked at Addie expectantly.

Chapter Six

"IT WAS A FEW DAYS ago," Addie said. "The mother and daughter came in, remember? Edna was the mother."

"Uh-huh, Edna and her daughter Heather," Chelsea said.

Addie nodded. Kate had finished her call and rejoined them.

"When they were coming in, Edna was complaining about 'the mayor's wife,'" Addie said. "She was actually pretty heated about it. She said something about how the mayor's wife had it out for them, and Edna swore she wouldn't let the woman get away with it, or something along those lines."

"Do you think Yuna was after Edna and Heather's donut shop, too?" Kate asked.

"Well, it would make sense," Addie said. "Donuts are similar to pastries. So if Lisette were trying to eliminate her competition, she would definitely want to go after Glazed."

Chelsea nodded and carefully printed "Edna and Heather Schmidt" on a blank page of her journal.

"Do you really think they're capable of poisoning Yuna, though?" she asked, looking up.

Addie shrugged. "I think anyone is capable of almost anything if they're desperate enough. It's motive, right?"

"It's hard for me to think of anyone in Stargaze capable of doing such a thing," Kate said, her blue eyes sad.

"Sometimes decent people do terrible things, though," Chelsea said quietly.

"It probably wasn't some rando out-of-town stranger," Addie pointed out. "A stranger has no reason to go to such lengths. At the very least, it had to be someone who knew Yuna."

They all contemplated that unpleasant thought for a moment.

"What about Yuna's husband?" Addie asked. "Could he have done it?"

Kate looked pained. "Oh, I just hate to think that."

Chelsea tapped her pen on her lower lip. "There have been some rumors about them."

"What kind of rumors?" Addie asked.

"Well, I heard he was going to file for divorce."

"Really," Addie said, loading the word with significance. She leaned forward. "I saw three prescription bottles in his gym bag. Maybe he drugged her." Her eyes popped wide. "Oh! Maybe he put drugs in her tincture. She would have noticed if he dropped anything in her wine, but he could have poisoned the bottle beforehand. And then when she took some of the tincture at dinner, which she must have because the bottle fell off the table and broke, she reacted to it."

"Possibly," Chelsea said. "I'm adding his name to the list."

"And we should figure out what was going on between the Akidos," Addie said.

"This is all so unsavory," Kate said, covering her eyes briefly.

A truck pulled up out front.

"I think Hank is here," Addie said.

An officer was parked out there, too. She tried to ignore the police cruiser, but she couldn't help wondering if she was going to be under surveillance. Helplessness washed over her anew.

"I'll call you with any news," Kate said as she went out the door.

"You know what, I'm not a prisoner here," Addie said after the truck pulled away. "And Lucky needs to go out. Want to take a walk with us?"

"Sure," Chelsea said, capping her pen.

They locked up the store and left with the little dog trotting between them. Addie ignored the police car.

"Glazed is a few blocks away, right?" she asked.

"Yeah," Chelsea said.

"Let's swing by there. Edna seems like a woman willing to talk about her problems to anyone who'll listen. Maybe we can learn something about her dealings with Yuna."

"Good idea."

Chelsea steered them toward the donut shop, which was on Mountain View Street, considered to be a prime location for Stargaze businesses. Pine Street, where Wild Rose and La Petite Patisserie were located, was seen as just off the prime area. Chelsea had told Addie that Lisette had originally wanted a more central location for her café, but Chelsea had actually won the bid for the space and opened a clothing boutique. Just one more reason Lisette held a grudge against Chelsea, and by extension against Addie.

The sun had set, and the late summer air was cooling. It felt nice to walk, and for a moment Addie could almost imagine that this was just a regular Sunday. But the tightness in her middle wouldn't let her forget that it was anything but a normal day.

Most of the businesses they passed were closed for the day.

"Oh, it looks dark," Chelsea said, pointing ahead.

Addie spotted the Glazed sign, which was in puffy white letters on a magenta background. The sign itself was dark, but the streetlamp on the corner provided substantial light.

They stopped, and Lucky looked up at them expectantly.

"Want to turn around?" Chelsea asked.

Addie nearly agreed to go back to Wild Rose when she thought she saw movement in the darkened donut shop. She moved against the brick building, which was still warm from the day, but did it casually, as there were still a few people and cars traversing the street.

"I think someone's in there," she whispered.

Chelsea moved next to her. Then the two of them sidled closer to the donut shop's window.

Addie faced Chelsea, as if they were in conversation, and then peered over Chelsea's shoulder into Glazed. Lucky came to sit on the sidewalk between them and looked up from one woman to the other, as if listening to their conversation.

"That's Heather. She's with someone. A man," Addie said.

Heather and the man were standing very close together in the far corner of the store where it was darkest. It was hard to see what was happening, but by their postures and small movements, Addie guessed they were deep in conversation. They were clearly very familiar with each other. She watched in silence for a moment, feeling a little guilty about spying. But if they wanted privacy, they shouldn't have been standing in a room with huge storefront windows facing one of the busiest streets in town.

"Who's the man?"

"I don't know," Addie said. "You look and see if you recognize him."

They shifted around so Chelsea could see inside.

She squinted. "That's . . . oh, I think that's the pharmacist from Westside Grocery on the other side of town." Her eyes widened. "Oh man, they're kissing. Like, kissing a *lot.*"

Addie leaned over to try to see. Just then, a light in the back room of the store came on, and the silhouette of someone on a motorized scooter—Edna Schmidt—appeared in the doorway. The pharmacist jumped away from Heather and disappeared down behind the counter. Heather walked swiftly toward her mother, and the scooter backed up. The two women disappeared into the back.

A moment later, the light went off. Heather came back to the front, moving in a hurry. The pharmacist popped up from where he'd been hiding. The two of them exchanged a few words, and then the man came toward the door.

"He's coming out the front," Addie murmured.

"Just act natural," Chelsea whispered. Then she started talking a little louder. "I was afraid that noise my car was making might be something serious, but then it cleared up on its own."

"Oh, yeah, that's good," Addie said. She watched as the pharmacist slipped out of Glazed, glanced both ways, and then began walking swiftly down the street. "Car repairs can be so expensive."

They went quiet for a moment until the pharmacist was well out of earshot.

Chelsea raised her brows.

"Someone's got a secret lover," she said in a singsong voice.

But Addie wasn't amused. She was remembering the bottles in the mayor's bag.

"Those prescription bottles came from the store that pharmacist works at," she said.

Chelsea shrugged. "Well, there are only like four pharmacies in town, so the odds were one in four."

"Yeah, but where do the Akidos live?" Addie asked. "Not west, I'm guessing. They both wore expensive clothes. She carried a designer bag."

"Huh, you're right," Chelsea said thoughtfully. "Their house is in the east hills."

The "east hills" of Stargaze were barely hills at all, really just low foothills that were enough above the rest of the town to give a view of Jade Lake. There were a couple of more expensive neighborhoods situated across the hills.

"Why would the mayor go all the way across town to get his prescriptions?" Addie wondered aloud.

"Maybe he's trying to hide something," Chelsea said.

"I think he is," Addie said, her brows knitting. "Most people wouldn't carry around three different pill bottles in a gym bag. Most people leave their prescriptions at home in the medicine cabinet, unless they're for something urgent or life-threatening. But what would be the odds of the mayor needing three different medications on hand at all times? He looked awfully healthy to me, and I'm guessing he's not much past forty years old."

"You know, it does seem odd," Chelsea agreed. "Let's file that away. Maybe it's nothing, but we'll keep it in mind in case it's not."

They walked back toward Wild Rose, and before they arrived, Kate called.

"Bennett was at home," she told Addie. "I explained what's going on, and he's following us back to the shop."

"That is wonderful news!" Addie said. "So, he's okay? Why wasn't he answering his phone?"

"Oh, right! I nearly forgot. He lost his phone a couple of days ago but was on the road and figured he'd wait until he got home to buy a new one. He just got back a couple of hours ago and hasn't gotten around to replacing it."

"I'm so glad that's all it was," Addie said. "I'll see you soon."

They arrived back at Wild Rose, beating Aunt Kate, Hank, and Bennett there. Addie was glad of that because it probably would have worried Kate to know Addie had left the store.

Officer Davis had taken over for the other policeman, and he stepped out of the cruiser.

"Would you be willing to give me your word that you'll stay in the rest of the night?" he asked Addie. "I'd really rather not have to sit out here. I'm hungry and my wife has dinner waiting. One of the other officers is supposed to relieve me in an hour, but he's got a sick baby at home, and I know he'd much rather be there. If I vouch for you, my boss will be okay with it."

"You'd trust my word?" Addie asked, arching a brow and wondering if it was a set-up. She doubted Detective McCann would ever be okay with such an arrangement.

The officer nodded. "I know your aunt, and she's got a heart of gold. She thinks so highly of you she's left you in charge of this shop, which is her life, while she's been unwell." He gestured at Wild Rose. "In my book, that means you're cut from the same cloth she is."

Addie's lips stretched in an unexpected smile, and she nearly teared up. "You don't know how nice that is to hear. I give you my word I'll be here until morning." She gave a firm nod. "Oh, unless Lucky has a potty emergency. But if that happens, I won't leave this block, I promise."

"Good enough for me," he said, giving her a warm smile that made him look like a young Morgan Freeman.

Addie felt a little better as the cruiser pulled away. At least someone beyond her aunt and friends didn't seem to think she was a murderer.

Hank's pickup arrived, and he waved as Kate got out. Then he drove off. Bennett rolled past in his Jeep Sahara, and Addie knew he was going to park at his office building and then walk back. It was the kind of thing Bennett would think of. The local police weren't fans of the town's private investigator, and being aware of that, Bennett would do his best to not make things more difficult for Addie.

While waiting for him, the three women decided it would be best to go upstairs and out of sight.

When Bennett arrived on foot, he gave Addie a broad smile and warm greeting, but his eyes seemed distant. After exchanging greetings, the four of them trooped upstairs with Lucky.

Kate went to start water in the electric kettle while Bennett began asking Addie questions. She answered all of them, and then she and Chelsea told him about their suspect list.

Addie realized they'd need to talk about their little stroll earlier that evening, too, and she cast a guilty look at Kate.

"Chelsea and I took a walk with Lucky," Addie said.

Kate turned from where she was setting mugs on the counter of the kitchenette. Her face reflected worry, but she didn't seem angry.

Addie and Chelsea recounted what they'd seen at Glazed, and Addie explained her hunch that the mayor might have poisoned his wife.

"Chelsea said there's a rumor they were splitting up," Addie said. Her gaze turned unfocused and thoughtful. "And come to think of it, the mayor reacted oddly when his wife collapsed. He reached out to try to help her, but he didn't seem as upset as the situation warranted."

Bennett leaned back in his chair. "I do know that Kenneth—that's the mayor's name—intended to file for divorce."

Addie's brows shot up.

"I came by that information while working for another client, so I'm not violating any confidentiality agreement," he added. "And it was going to be a messy one. He's got some family money."

"Wow, okay," Chelsea said. "That could be considered motive, right?"

"It could," Bennett said. He cocked his head, his gaze sliding up to a corner of the room. "But if Kenneth did it, why would he choose to have it happen in such a public way? That seems unnecessarily messy and . . . dramatic."

"But when there's foul play, it's often someone very close to the victim, right?" Addie asked.

"Often, yes," Bennett said. "And money does often play a part. I want to look into who else Yuna might have had it out for in her capacity as a health inspector. It seems like an angle we shouldn't eliminate quite yet."

Addie gave her head a slight shake. It made a lot more sense to her that a husband wanting to get rid of his wife would be the one to poison her rather than a disgruntled business owner going to all that trouble. Yuna might have caused a lot of problems for Stargaze proprietors, but to the point of murder? It just seemed awfully extreme to Addie.

It irked her the tiniest bit that Bennett didn't see it the same way. She thought he was headed off in the wrong direction, but he was offering to help, and she needed all the support she could get.

They talked for a few more minutes, and then Chelsea and Bennett left and Hank came to get Kate.

Addie was still stressed but was comforted by Bennett's return and the support of her aunt and best friend.

Exhausted and cautiously hopeful, she fell asleep easily.

It was the last peaceful night's sleep she would get, though, because things were about to go terribly awry.

Chapter Seven

THE NEXT MORNING, KATE ARRIVED before Wild Rose opened so she could help Addie with the morning checklist and attend to some other things around the shop.

Addie knew Kate felt badly about being gone a lot and leaning so much on her niece, not to mention partly responsible for the mess with the police over Yuna Akido's death.

It was a comfort to have Kate there, and Addie was almost able to push her worries aside as she focused on the shop duties. But the back of her mind was still working on the idea that Kenneth Akido had killed his wife.

Bennett stopped by briefly to let Kate and Addie know that he planned to question some of the witnesses who'd been present when Yuna collapsed at dinner, as well as dig into what was going on between the Akidos and anything else that might help Addie's cause.

"That's a huge amount of work," Addie said. "We need a formal contract this time."

But he held up his hand, shaking his head in refusal. "We'll have the same arrangement as last time. My fee is a dollar, and I'll send you the paperwork."

"No," Addie insisted. "This is more than just a favor. This is a full-scale investigation."

But Bennett wouldn't hear of it.

Aunt Kate passed him a one-dollar bill, and he made his escape with Addie still calling out her protests after him.

She turned, her hands on her hips, to face Aunt Kate.

"I appreciate his help," Addie said. "But I can't let him do this. Even if I don't have the cash, I'll put it on credit cards or—or take out a loan or something. This is too much."

Kate gave a gentle smile, her blue eyes sparkling. "Oh, pish posh," she said with a dismissive wave of her hand. "He wants to help you, and if he truly needed the money, he'd charge you. I say let him do it."

Addie shook her head. "No, I need to do something for him."

"Dinner," Kate said.

"Make him dinner?"

"No, just say yes to dinner with him."

"But he hasn't asked me to dinner," Addie said, wrinkling her nose in confusion.

"He will."

Addie just peered at Kate for a minute, unsure of what to say to that. But there wasn't much time to consider it, as the first customer of the day had arrived, a woman looking for a special tea to serve to her book club later that week.

Aunt Kate created a custom tea formulation while Addie took Lucky down the block and back.

There was no cruiser parked out front, and that seemed a good sign. Maybe the case had gone a different direction and Addie was no longer under suspicion.

When she got back to Wild Rose, she had an email from Bennett with a link to sign a contract that made his work for her official. He also texted to let her know he'd gotten a new phone.

Later in the day, a familiar face appeared in the shop.

"Hello, dearie," Betty called out to Addie as she came in.

Kate emerged from the back and exchanged greetings with her longtime friend.

Betty came to lean her forearms on the counter, clasping her plump hands together. Her nails were painted a deep sparkly purple that matched her eyeshadow.

"Have you had a chance to look at the book?" Betty asked.

"I'm sorry. I haven't," Addie said. "I've been really wrapped up the past few days. You heard about Yuna?"

"Yes," Betty said solemnly. "And I saw the cruiser out front and the detective come and go."

Addie slumped against the counter. "It seems I'm on their short list of suspects because I made a tincture for Yuna the day before she died." She went on to describe all the reasons why it didn't make sense that she would be a suspect. "I'm hoping that the absence of the police car means they've come to their senses."

Betty's eyes, large and brown, were serious and unblinking.

"Well, dearie, I wouldn't count on that, unfortunately," she said quietly.

Addie frowned. "Why?"

"I did a tarot spread for you this morning, one focused specifically on this situation," Betty said. "And it was very clear that things are going to get worse before they get better. I'm sorry, dearie. I know that's not what you want to hear."

Irritation flared through Addie, but she did her best to tamp it down.

But a *tarot* reading? Really? Betty had come over to upset Addie over what a few silly cards supposedly were saying?

"Hm," Addie said, carefully neutral. "What do you suggest I do?"

"Consult the leaves, Addie," Betty said. "Do a reading. I'll come to be with you while you do it, if you want. I know it's a bit unsettling. I'll try to help you with the interpretation, too, if I can."

"Maybe later," Addie said, forcing a small smile.

Betty straightened. "Okay, dearie. All you have to do is give a holler, and Betty will do what she can to help you."

"Thank you. I appreciate the offer," Addie said and then turned away before she allowed her impatience to show.

Kate had been watching and listening quietly. Addie caught her gaze and gave her aunt a wide-eyed look of frustration. Neither of them spoke until Betty was gone.

"I know she's just trying to help," Addie said, holding up a hand in defense of what she knew Aunt Kate was thinking. "I just don't find her help very *helpful*. In any case, now I'm not as worried. We haven't seen an officer or a detective all day. I'm not even sure we need Bennett anymore."

"I'm sure you're right," Kate said with a smile. But the tension didn't completely leave her eyes.

The next few hours were routine, with a continuing stream of customers.

A couple of hours before closing time, Bennett came in.

Addie started to smile in greeting but then caught sight of his expression. He didn't just look grim; he looked stricken.

"What's wrong?" Addie asked, alarm gripping her stomach.

Bennett glanced at the man paying for a gift tin of tea for his wife and waited a few seconds for the man to depart.

"I have a connection in the medical examiner's office," Bennett said. "And I just got word from her that the contents of Yuna's stomach have been analyzed."

"And?" Kate asked, coming to stand next to Addie.

"It appears she drank from her wine glass and her water glass at the restaurant," he said. "She also took some of the tincture. And there was an additional substance dissolved in her stomach, a narcotic pain reliever called fentanyl. Obviously enough to be fatal."

Addie's chest seemed to restrict as she forced out the question racing through her mind: "Can they tell if the fentanyl was mixed into the tincture?"

Bennett shook his head. "Not conclusively."

"Maybe she just took too much of it," Kate suggested. "What is it, anyway?"

"It's a narcotic pain reliever," Bennett said. "But the problem is, no one would knowingly take that much. She had many times the safe dose in her system."

"Do we know if she had a prescription for fentanyl?" Kate asked.

"I don't know the answer to that at this point," he said.

"Her husband had three pill bottles in his gym bag that night at La Petite Patisserie," Addie said. She told him the name of the pharmacy on the prescription labels. "I only got a look at two of them, and I don't think either of them said fentanyl. But the third might have."

Bennett nodded. "I'm going to look into that. It's not easy to get information related to people's medical records, but I'll do what I can."

Addie examined his face. "But this is somehow bad news for me, isn't it?" she asked quietly.

"It looks that way," Bennett said, his eyes almost mournful.

"But why?"

"At least two witnesses saw her take liquid from the tincture bottle right before she collapsed," Bennett said. "From what I've learned, no one saw her take any pills."

"She could have taken them right before she arrived, though."

"Maybe, but the medical examiner thinks the tincture, wine, and fentanyl were all ingested within several minutes of each other. Or possibly the fentanyl was dissolved in one of the substances. And like I said, it was a very large dose. She wouldn't have taken a handful of these pills if she had a prescription for them."

Addie felt the blood drain from her face. Suddenly feeling unsteady, she pressed both palms onto the counter.

"I don't even have access to narcotics," Addie said, her voice faint. Feeling her panic starting to gain momentum again, she forced her thoughts to focus and looked at Bennett. "I still say her husband slipped them into her tincture."

"Like I said, I'm going to try to get some info on his prescriptions," Bennett said. "But it's protected by privacy laws, so it won't be easy, unless he's willing to offer up the information freely."

And if Kenneth Akido killed his wife, why in the world would he do that?

"Bennett, am I going to be arrested?" Addie asked.

"I'm not sure, Addie," he said, and then his mouth settled into a grim line for a moment. "But I do know the local government is putting a lot of pressure on the police to get a suspect behind bars. As you probably know, the festival season is about to begin, and the city of Stargaze doesn't want the poisoning of a high-profile citizen hanging over us. A wholesome reputation is our hallmark, and the local economy is heavily dependent on tourists coming for the festivals."

"Oh my, no," Kate said, a hand on her chest. "Do you really think they would rush an arrest just to try to get the whole thing wrapped up?"

"I wouldn't rule that out," Bennett said.

Addie pinched the bridge of her nose and squeezed her eyes closed as a headache began to pulse in her temples.

The news just seemed to be getting worse and worse.

She looked up. "And let me guess, the mayor has connections with the police? Connections that will help him deflect suspicion from himself?"

"Kenneth's cousin in the Chief of Police," Bennett said. "I wasn't going to bring it up, but there you have it."

"Of course," she murmured, staring out the front window of the shop.

Stargaze had always been her favorite place in the world, with Wild Rose Teas and Apothecary being at the heart of her love for this place.

But now, it felt as if danger and betrayal lurked on every sunny street corner.

"Addie," Bennett said, waiting until her gaze met his to continue. "We're going to figure this out. You're not going to take the blame for Yuna Akido's death."

Kate came to touch Addie's upper back, tracing slow, comforting lines back and forth.

"Bennett's right," Aunt Kate said. "Things look ugly now, but the real murderer *will* be caught. Don't lose your trust in people doing the right thing."

"Okay, I'll try," Addie said, nodding. "But I need something to do. There's just too much for Bennett to try to do it all, anyway. Too many people to talk to, too much to figure out."

"How about if I come back after closing tonight and we can get specific about who does what?" Bennett suggested.

Addie smiled in relief, as she'd been afraid he might tell her to leave everything to him.

"I'm sure Chelsea will help," she said.

"Betty, too," Kate said. She bit her bottom lip for a moment. "And . . . there's something . . . *unique*, but possibly helpful, I might be able to do, too."

A significant glance passed between Aunt Kate and Bennett, but Addie wasn't quite sure what it meant.

"Okay, I should get going," Bennett said in a businesslike tone, rapping his knuckles sharply on the countertop. "I'll see you this evening."

Addie took a breath and faced her aunt. "Maybe—maybe I should try to do a tea-leaf reading."

"Wouldn't hurt to try. Shall I boil some water?"

"Sure," Addie said. "If you can keep an eye on the shop, I'll go upstairs to do it."

While Kate started the electric kettle, Addie got a cup and saucer and then stood before the large glass jars of tea.

It probably didn't matter much which tea she chose, but she wanted it to be something she liked, at least. After a moment of consideration, she reached for the peppermint that she and Kate and Chelsea had sipped together. Peppermint was a strong scent and flavor, one that tended to cut through all else with a signature clarity. It was comforting and refreshing, but also no-nonsense, and that somehow seemed fitting.

Addie dropped a generous pinch of tea straight into the cup, filled it halfway with hot water, and carried it upstairs.

In the apartment, she sat at the tiny dining table with Lucky curled up at her feet. As she sipped, she contemplated her situation and silently asked for guidance in discovering Yuna's murderer.

Once she was down to just a bit of liquid and saturated peppermint leaves, she swirled the cup and turned it over onto the saucer.

Pausing for a moment, she took a steadying breath. Then she turned the saucer right side up and peered into it.

Some of the soggy peppermint was still clumped in the bottom of the cup, while some had streaked the sides. A small chunk balanced on the rim.

Addie's mind began to whirl, and dizziness started to sweep over her. Before it could grow too intense, she quickly took a picture of the cup with her phone.

A tingling sensation began to take root in the center of her chest, growing until it felt like a swarm of bees. The tingling burst outward through her body, and Addie gasped and pressed her hands onto the table.

Her vision began to blur, and her breath came faster.

With her heart racing, she tried to steady her nerves and focus on the tea leaves. Her vision sharpened, and what had looked like random blobs of wet peppermint took on dimension. Lines began to form, like details being drawn in by a skilled and steady hand.

She concentrated, taking it all in with a single-minded focus. A whisper began to grow in the center of her mind, but it was too soft to pick out any words.

Just as she began to pick out distinct shapes, voices downstairs distracted her. She tried to block it out, but her aunt's voice cut through the vision, and Addie's mind tuned into the alarm in Kate's tone.

"—making a mistake," Aunt Kate was saying. "It's just not possible."

There were footsteps on the stairs.

Addie looked to see who it was, and the trance was broken. The whisper silenced, and the tingling cut off so abruptly Addie inhaled sharply through her nose.

Aunt Kate came into view, and her face was a mask of shock.

Behind her came Officer Davis and Detective McCann.

Kate was still protesting. Addie stared in confusion, and dread began to curl through her.

"Addison James, could you please stand up?" Officer Davis said, his eyes full of regret.

"What's going on?" Addie asked, slowly rising.

Lucky let out a low growl, and she weakly shushed him.

"Ms. James, we've come to arrest you for the murder of Yuna Akido," Detective McCann said.

Chapter Eight

ADDIE FORGOT TO BREATHE AS Officer Davis came closer.

"If you'll come with me quietly and get into the cruiser, I won't have to cuff you," he said.

She could see in his eyes that this was causing him pain. He didn't think she'd killed Yuna. Or, at least, he wanted to believe she hadn't.

"But what evidence do you have?" Aunt Kate demanded, looking back and forth between Officer Davis and Detective McCann.

Kate's eyes were getting bloodshot, some part of Addie's mind noticed.

"Enough evidence to get a warrant for Addison's arrest," McCann said.

"The evidence is wrong," Addie said, her voice hoarse. "Anything tying me to this is weak at best."

"I'm going to start reading you your rights," Officer Davis said. "Then we'll need to go. You should bring ID with you; it'll make things a little easier at the station."

"You're *wrong*," Addie insisted, pleading with the officer. "Have you even looked at her husband? He's got a bunch of prescriptions!" Her voice was getting shrill, and it almost felt like it was coming from somewhere else. "He was going to divorce her! He's got motive, don't you see that?"

Kate found Addie's driver license and then came over to take her arm, trying to soothe her and also gently guide her toward the stairs. Lucky's anxious whines provided a backdrop to it all. Kate slid the ID into Addie's front pocket.

"Shh," Kate said. "Don't say anything more, okay, honey?"

Aunt Kate hadn't called Addie "honey" in years.

"But I'm not—" Addie started to protest.

"I know," Kate cut her off. "And others know it too. We're going to clear this up. But for now, you'll have to go with them."

Officer Davis finished reciting the Miranda rights that up to that point Addie had only ever heard on TV shows. Those detective shows where they always got the right bad guy.

Kate wrapped her arm tightly around Addie's shoulder, and they walked down the stairs side by side.

"Call Bennett," Addie said. "Will you?"

"Of course." Kate squeezed her shoulder. "Do your best to stay calm, and we'll see about bail."

Bail?

Then it really started to sink in.

They're taking me to jail.

"Lucky," Addie whispered. "Please take care of him."

"He'll be fine here. I promise," Kate said. "And so excited to see you when you come home."

In a daze, Addie walked through the store and out the front door with Officer Davis going ahead and Detective McCann behind.

The detective gave some papers to Kate. Maybe a copy of the arrest warrant? Addie almost asked for it, but then she realized she wouldn't be able to take anything in with her.

Outside, Officer Davis held open the back door of his cruiser.

With a moan of misery trying to rise up her throat, Addie climbed into the back seat. The door slammed and she jumped and blinked, the noise snapping her out of her daze to some extent.

She looked back at Aunt Kate as Officer Davis started up the police car, pulled from the curb, and flipped a U-turn. They went right past La Petite Patisserie, where Lisette stood at the counter watching the cruiser go by. Her gaze locked with Addie's for a split second before the cruiser turned left, and Lisette's look of smug satisfaction was unmistakable.

"What's going to happen?" Addie asked anxiously, knowing that Officer Davis would be helpful if he could, and she had no idea who'd she be dealing with at the police station.

There was a small jail at the station, which Addie had actually visited before when she was trying to unravel the mystery of who had attacked and nearly killed Aunt Kate.

"Well, we'll process you, and you'll be spending the night with us at the station," he said.

"I can't get out on bail?" she asked, her voice small.

He shook his head and glanced at her in the rearview while they were at a stoplight.

"No, not right away," he said. "There will have to be a bail hearing, where the amount will be set."

Addie's heart plummeted. "How long will that take?"

"It'll happen tomorrow, most likely," he replied. "Usually around here, we can get bail hearings within twenty-four hours of arrests."

Arrests.

Even if the charges were dropped later, Addie would have an *arrest record*. The realization made her sick to her stomach, and the smell of the cruiser didn't help matters. There was a sickly strong scent of disinfectant and under that something acrid. Addie shifted on the seat, not wanting to think about what kind of messes might have been cleaned off it. At least Officer Davis had both front windows down all the way.

"Do you think I'm guilty, Officer?" Addie asked.

"That's not for me to determine," he said. There was a long pause before he added, "But you certainly don't strike me as a killer, Ms. James."

"Apparently someone thinks there's ample evidence to treat me like one," Addie said, not trying to hide the bitterness in her voice.

"I believe the right person will be punished," he said, and the implication was clear that he didn't think Addie was the right suspect.

She got some comfort from that. But considering she was minutes away from jail, the comfort was short-lived.

McCann met them at the station, where they walked her inside.

They did some paperwork while Addie emptied her pockets—placing her phone, driver's license, and a dog treat on a tray at the request of an officer with large, slightly bulging eyes and a horseshoe ring of close-cropped dark-brown hair.

She was surprisingly relieved to find she'd be able to keep her own clothes on. The idea of putting on a bright-orange jailhouse jumpsuit was somehow too awful to think about.

The officer processing her took her fingerprints, too, all the while barely even glancing at Addie, as if he saw criminals like her so often it didn't even phase him.

He took her mug shot, and once the processing was done, she was escorted through a security door.

Addie had been back there before with Aunt Kate to confront a man who'd been new in town. His shop, Ripped, had been situated across the street between Hair Affair and Betty's emporium. He'd been the one who'd attacked Kate and nearly killed her.

This time, Addie was on the other side of things, and the sight of the barred cells somehow felt a lot more shocking knowing she was going to be contained within one of them.

The processing officer keyed open the first cell on the left and waited for her to go in. Setting her jaw and promising herself this was only temporary, Addie walked in. The balding officer slid the door closed with a resonant clang and locked it with a key from his large, heavy-looking ring.

Addie was alone in the cell.

With her hands on her hips, she took in her surroundings, forcing herself to stay as detached as possible.

Pretend this is an experiment. Make observations.

Metal bunkbed along the left concrete wall, each with a thin rubber mattress that reminded her of the tumble pads from elementary school gym class. The pads were in good repair and looked clean.

Industrial linoleum floor that was mostly brown, except for a couple of navy-blue tiles that appeared newer than the brown ones. The floor sloped toward the corridor that ran between two rows of cells, and drains dotted the corridor's floor.

There was a metal partition at the back wall, and a peek behind it revealed a stainless-steel toilet and sink. At least if she needed to use the facilities there was enough privacy to do so. That was actually a huge relief.

The other two walls were barred, and the one on the right had a five-foot gap between it and the barred wall of the cell next door.

There was no window, and the ceiling was about fifteen feet high.

All-in-all, it was much cleaner and less spartan than she'd imagined.

She went to sit on the lower bunk with a sigh.

One other cell was occupied—the last one on the other side of the corridor—and the man in it appeared to have passed out on the bed, where he was snoring loudly.

Addie turned her hands palms up, looking down at her fingertips, which had just been pressed against a sensor that electronically recorded her fingerprints.

She was now "in the system." An arrestee.

Fear and helplessness started to seep through her like a cold tide, but she pushed them down.

She couldn't go anywhere, but she still had her mind, and she had the memory of what she'd seen in the tea leaves before she'd been interrupted.

There hadn't been time for all of the images to fully form, but she'd gotten some partial pictures in the soggy peppermint.

She closed her eyes and slowed her breathing, taking measured inhales and longer exhales. After a minute or so, she felt surprisingly calm.

It was time to examine what she'd seen.

One of the images had been very distinct: two snakes twisting around a vertical line that had small wings at the top.

It was a symbol of medicine and healing. Yuna had essentially overdosed on a prescription drug. Did the symbol mean the drug had come from a doctor rather than the black market? It seemed a reasonable guess.

In her mind's eye, she moved on to another tiny image in the tea leaves.

This one was also unmistakable—a dollar sign.

Bennett had said that money was often a motive, and Addie took the dollar sign to be confirmation of that.

Kenneth Akido had wanted to divorce his wife, and Bennett indicated there was going to be a battle over money. The dollar sign seemed to support Addie's theory that Kenneth had murdered Yuna to avoid a messy divorce where his family money would have been at risk. Plus, divorces were expensive, so even if Kenneth had won in the end and not had to fork over some of his inheritance, he surely would have ended up paying some serious cash for lawyer fees.

Okay, so those were two clues from the tea that seemed to point to Kenneth as the murderer.

What else had the leaves shown?

Addie concentrated, trying to bring up the details.

There'd been two other tiny pictures. One was a series of little O's. And the other was . . . a grouping of squiggles and lines.

She made an impatient noise in the back of her throat.

She'd gotten disrupted before she could focus much on the squiggles and lines, and she wasn't even sure she remembered that symbol accurately.

Standing, she paced slowly from one side of the cell to the other and back again, hoping the movement would help her think.

Were the tiny circles symbolic of the pills?

She wasn't sure what fentanyl pills looked like. Many pills were oblong, but some were round tablets.

Maybe the circles weren't pills.

So, what did the circles mean?

Deciding she might as well get comfortable, Addie stretched out with her hands behind her head, pondering her disrupted tea-leaf vision.

After maybe fifteen minutes had passed, she realized she'd been so focused for a while she'd forgotten to be scared.

Well, that was something, anyway.

She sat up and swung her legs to the floor when she heard the outer security door clang closed. Someone stopped at her cell.

"Officer Davis," she said. "I don't suppose you found the real suspect and you're here to let me go?"

He gave her a kind grin. "Unfortunately, not yet." He lifted his hands, one of which held a plastic liter bottle of water and the other a Subway bag. "I thought you might like a bite to eat, though."

He'd brought her a sandwich. In jail. The gesture nearly made her cry.

"That is so kind of you," she said around a small lump in her throat. She went to where he stood. "Thank you so much."

She wasn't particularly hungry, but she would be at some point.

He passed the items through the bars. Holding the bottle and sack felt so wonderfully normal she couldn't help feeling a little better.

"Any word on when I might have my bail hearing?" she asked.

"There was a last-minute schedule change, so there's an opening first thing in the morning. Eight sharp. I'll come and get you and take you to the courthouse."

"Oh wow, that's really fortunate," she said, knowing she was extremely lucky to not have to wait longer.

"I know this isn't exactly the Ritz Carlton," he said. "But I hope you'll be able to get a little shut-eye tonight."

"I'll do my best," she said, mostly to reassure him.

"Okay, then. I'll see you in the morning."

"Goodnight, Officer Davis."

He departed, leaving her with her dinner and the snores of the inmate down the hall.

She paced around the cell for a while, trying to work off some of her anxiety, and continued to think about the murder.

Was Bennett making any headway with his investigation into Kenneth Akido?

Her thoughts then turned to her bail hearing. How high would the amount be set? Aunt Kate would want to get Addie out of jail, of course, but Kate wasn't a wealthy woman. Her shop was reasonably successful in that she turned a profit, but it wasn't exactly a gold mine. What if she didn't have enough for bail?

Addie sagged onto the lower bunk, her worries swirling.

Realizing she'd probably feel better if she ate, she opened the Subway bag and found a ham-and-cheese sub with tomatoes, lettuce, and mayo. There was a bag of Doritos, too. Gratitude swept through her anew.

Once she'd finished the food and downed a third of the water, she rolled up the bag with the wrappers inside it. She had started to zone out on the tea-leaf images again when the security door popped open.

Three men came through. One of them was dressed in slacks and a sport jacket, and the other two wore dress pants and button-down shirts.

They stopped in front of her cell.

"This is her," said the one in the sport jacket.

Addie did a double-take when she looked into his eyes. He had the same straight brow and pointed chin as Kenneth Akido.

This man had to be the police chief that Bennett had mentioned.

"Huh," one of the other two men said, regarding her as if she were an animal in the zoo. "Daughter of some woo-woo herbal lady or something, right?"

"Niece," the chief corrected.

Addie rose and walked toward where they stood.

"Excuse me, what is it you're here for?" she asked.

The chief gave her a stony look. "Just wanted to get a look at the suspect."

Hot anger boiled up through Addie.

He was trying to intimidate her by treating her as if she were just an object in a box.

"You must be the chief of police," she said, returning his cold stare. Then her gaze shifted to the two other men as she folded her arms. "And who are you?"

One of them opened his mouth, seemingly ready to give his name, but the chief held up a hand. "She doesn't need to know that. Let's go to my office where we can talk."

They turned, and still talking about her as if she wasn't even there, one of the men asked, "So there's enough to convict?"

She just caught the first part of the chief's reply as the security door closed: "We'll make sure of that. We've gotta get this buttoned up real soon; that's priority one, and everyone is on board with—"

Addie didn't hear the rest, but the entire encounter was enough to leave her heart racing with pent-up anger.

Bennett was right, it seemed. They just needed someone to pin the murder on so the fall festival season wouldn't be affected by bad press.

The way they'd looked at her and spoken to her was both humiliating and horrifying. They didn't really care if she was guilty or not. They didn't care what happened to her.

Narrowing her eyes, Addie gripped the bars harder and harder until her knuckles went bloodless.

She was *not* going down for Yuna Akido's murder.

Chapter Nine

ADDIE DOZED FITFULLY THROUGHOUT THE night, not really sleeping but not really awake either. The next morning—at least she assumed it was morning when the dimmed lights came on fully—arrived with a sour taste in her mouth and grogginess fogging her brain.

She sat up, stiff from sleeping on the hard mat, and took a deep breath.

She'd made it through a night in jail. That counted for something, didn't it? Certainly an item to add to the Things I Never Thought I'd Do list.

After splashing some water on her face in the small stainless-steel sink, patting her skin dry with her sleeve, and swishing some bottled water around in her mouth, she paced around the cell to try to loosen her stiff back.

It had to be almost time to head to the courthouse for the bail hearing. She wished she had a mirror and a brush, and maybe a fresh shirt, but those were conveniences beyond her reach for the moment.

She'd had to relinquish her hair elastic when she'd been processed, so she finger-combed her long auburn hair and then smoothed it back into a braid, using the ends of her hair to tie a little knot to keep the braid in place. Then, dampening her hands, she tried to smooth the front of the somewhat wrinkled zip-up jacket she wore over her t-shirt.

There. That was the best she could do.

Just in time, too, as the security door buzzed open and in walked Officer Davis.

"'Morning," he said. "I'm guessing you're ready to get out of here."

"You have no idea," Addie said. "And do you ever sleep?"

"I've been working a lot of overtime to save up for a big family vacation," he said.

She went for the bottle and Subway bag, but he indicated she should leave those things in the cell.

He held up a set of metal cuffs. "You're going to have to wear these lovely bracelets to court," he said.

Addie's mouth twisted. Not because she was afraid of being handcuffed but because she knew the cuffs would just make her look more like a criminal.

"Well, I do prefer silver to gold," she quipped, making Officer Davis smile.

He unlocked the door and slid it aside with a clang.

"Hands in front, please," he said. "It's a lot more comfortable that way."

She stuck her arms out and watched, almost as if observing from afar, as he clicked the metal rings around her wrists.

Her bravado faltered for a second, and she was afraid she might start tearing up, but Officer Davis took her arm.

"Allow me to escort you," he said jauntily.

She managed a little laugh.

They went back out the way she'd come in and stopped briefly at the processing desk to collect some papers from a different officer, this one a woman of about fifty with sharp, bird-like features and a short bob that hugged her head like a dark-brown helmet.

Officer Davis kept a light hold on Addie's arm as he took her out to his car.

Once she was settled in the back and he was behind the wheel, she leaned forward a bit to speak to him.

"The police chief and a couple of other guys came in last night," she said.

His gaze sharpened on her in the rearview mirror. "Is that so?"

She nodded. "It was . . . weird. Do you know who the two other men were?" She briefly described them.

"Sounds like a couple of lawyer friends of Chief Clemmens." His tone was carefully neutral, but Addie saw his mouth purse in distaste.

"Great," she mumbled and slumped back in the seat.

"How was it weird?"

She described the encounter, trying her best to put into words how she'd felt like a zoo animal on display.

"Huh," Officer Davis said. "That does sound uncomfortable."

He had to be careful what he said, of course. Chief Clemmens was Officer Davis's boss. But by his reaction, she sensed there was something that didn't sit right with him.

They soon arrived at a small municipal building on the south side of town.

Addie's heart lifted as they passed the parking lot and she spotted Aunt Kate's Subaru and Chelsea's yellow VW bug.

Officer Davis drove around to the back of the building and parked in a spot reserved for police cars.

She blinked in the bright morning sun as he guided her to a door labeled "Inmate Entrance."

Ugh. *Inmate*.

Addie couldn't wait to leave that label behind.

Her pulse began to speed up as they went through the security check and Officer Davis handed over some paperwork to a male clerk who sat behind a pane of thick glass.

"You can go in," the clerk said, pointing to a door. "Judge Manderley is in his office, and the courtroom is open."

Addie's body prickled with a nervous, cold sweat.

Would the judge be harsh? Would the bail be something she and Aunt Kate could manage? Would Addie even *get* bail? She suddenly remembered police procedural shows where the crime was so serious the accused wasn't even allowed out on bail. "Held without bail," or something, wasn't that the phrase?

Please, please don't let that happen.

"Take a deep breath," Officer Davis whispered to her as he took her to the door the clerk had pointed to. "Let it out slow."

Addie nodded, too nervous to speak.

Inside the courtroom, there were two people in the area in front of the raised desk where the judge would sit—a clean-cut young man sitting in front of one of those odd little court typewriters and a frizzy-haired woman at a desk tapping away on a laptop.

Officer Davis led Addie toward another woman, who turned and rose. She was dressed in a dark-green skirt and matching blazer with a white blouse underneath.

"Addison James?" she asked with a small, businesslike smile.

"Uh, yes," Addie said.

The back door opened, and Aunt Kate and Chelsea walked in. Addie's knees wobbled in relief at the sight of friendly faces. But the business-suit woman was talking, so Addie tried to keep her focus on what the lady was saying.

"I'm Maureen Kaposky," she said. "Your aunt hired me to represent you."

"Oh," Addie said, her brows lifting. "Oh! Well, thank you."

Officer Davis went to sit on a bench at the wall.

A harried-looking man in a rumpled brown suit came in through a side door on the opposite wall, carrying some folders in one hand and a briefcase in the other.

"That's the county prosecutor," Maureen murmured.

Addie tensed, suddenly realizing she was looking at the man whose job it was to try to put her in prison.

Then another officer walked in.

"Rise," he said.

Everyone in the courtroom who wasn't already standing did so.

The officer—the bailiff, Addie guessed—sat on a chair near the frizzy-haired woman.

And then Judge Manderley came in through the back door, his black robe sweeping around him as he shut the door and faced the courtroom.

"Be seated," he said.

He had salt-and-pepper hair with a neat, short beard to match. Addie guessed he was maybe mid-sixties.

The laptop lady—maybe the judge's assistant?—announced Addie's case.

And then the lawyers started talking.

In a daze, Addie tried to follow what they were saying. The prosecutor gave his bail recommendation, and Addie's heart skipped a beat as she processed the number.

It wasn't a million dollars, thank goodness. But it was a *lot*.

Maureen then stood and argued for a lower number.

The prosecutor protested. "This is a killing, your honor. And the accused has access, though her job at, uh"—he paused to consult his notes on a yellow pad—"Wild Rose Teas and Apothecary to druglike substances. She can't be allowed to continue to peddle these things to the public when she's been accused of poisoning her wares."

The judge nodded, seemingly in agreement.

"But your honor," Maureen protested. "The evidence is barely circumstantial. This is a very weak case, really. Plus, Ms. James has no prior record and no known criminal activity. Her last brush with the law was a speeding ticket over five years ago." She gave the judge a smile. "She's a model citizen."

Addie held her breath, waiting for the judge's reaction and the prosecutor's argument.

The man in the brown suit started his rebuttal, but the judge held up a hand.

"Thank you both," Judge Manderley said, cutting off the prosecutor. "I've reviewed what we have, and I agree that it's not a strong case at this point."

Addie tensed. Would he dismiss the charge? *Could* he dismiss it?

"But due to the seriousness of the crime, some measures must be taken while the investigation is ongoing," he continued. "I'm willing to set bail, but only if the defendant doesn't step foot in the establishment for the duration of this case. Additionally, the county requests that the business remain closed during that time as well."

Addie blinked, trying to understand where he was going.

There was a bit more haggling. Maureen held firm on keeping Wild Rose open, arguing that Kate James, as the owner, didn't deserve the financial hardship caused by events she hadn't been involved with. The prosecutor agreed to an amount for bail and agreed to let Kate keep the shop open, but he still insisted that Addie had to stay away from Wild Rose Teas and Apothecary. In addition, she was not to have access to any of the items in the business.

A couple of minutes later, the judge had ruled, and then they were finished.

Maureen turned to Addie. "I know you live above the store, but for now you'll have to find a different place to stay," the attorney said.

"I'm sure my friend Chelsea Spring will let me stay with her," Addie said. "But that's a lot of money. I don't know if Aunt Kate and I can come up with that much."

"She and I talked briefly," Maureen said. "It sounds like she and your friend have a plan."

The bailiff took Addie back to the processing area where she'd entered with Officer Davis.

"You can wait there," he said, pointing to a bench.

She wasn't totally sure what was happening but hoped she wasn't going to have to return to the county jail.

When she spotted Aunt Kate and Chelsea coming down the opposite hallway, Addie's heart leapt. Maureen was with them, and she came to sit next to Addie.

"Things are slow here today," Maureen said. "So, they're going to go ahead and get the bail taken care of."

"They are?" Addie watched her aunt and friend.

Last night, Chelsea and Kate must have put some real effort into figuring out what they'd do about Addie's bail. They clearly wanted to save Addie as much discomfort as possible. Her eyes misted with gratitude, and she swallowed hard. She just hoped Aunt Kate wasn't going to have to sell the business or anything drastic like that.

"Whatever gets put up for my bail will be returned to them, right?" Addie asked.

"As long as you don't violate the terms," Maureen said. "Definitely don't leave the city limits. You don't want to look like you were trying to flee the area."

"Oh, I won't," Addie promised.

"In the paperwork, you'll need to declare where you'll be residing," she said.

Addie nodded, watching her aunt.

Kate and Chelsea both gave encouraging smiles, and Addie managed to smile back.

"We have to go talk to a different clerk to get this done," Kate called over. "We'll be back."

"I'm going to stay here with you," Maureen said.

"Thanks. I really appreciate everything you've done."

"Well, we're not finished yet. If we go to trial, there's going to be a whole lot of work to do."

Trial?

Addie's stomach seemed to drop through the floor.

Would it really come to that?

No, just *no*. She couldn't allow her mind to go there.

Straightening, she squared her shoulders. "There's not going to be a trial," she said firmly. "It's not going to go that far because I didn't do it."

Maureen held up her hands. "I'm here to represent you. I don't determine guilt or innocence."

"You really think I did it?" Addie asked incredulously.

"I'm your lawyer. My opinions and judgments about you and your actions aren't part of our relationship."

Addie had liked Maureen at first but couldn't help feeling a little soured on the attorney after that kind of comment.

"It'll be a short relationship, then, because there's no way I'm going to prison for a crime I didn't do," Addie said. "No offense, but I don't intend to be working with you for long."

Before the attorney could reply, Kate and Chelsea appeared again, this time hurrying toward Addie.

"We have it!" Chelsea said triumphantly waving some papers.

She went up to the bailiff, who reviewed her paperwork. Then he came over to Addie.

"I can take those off you now," he said. "You're free to leave with your aunt."

Addie just about did a little dance in her seat. When her hands were free, she threw her arms around her aunt and then her friend.

Tears leaked from Addie's eyes. "I don't know how I can ever repay you for this."

Chelsea linked her arm through Addie's. "Let's worry about that later. First, we need to get out of here."

"I agree," Addie said.

She almost expected someone to try to stop her as she left the building. But no one did. She rode with Aunt Kate.

"I'm going to take you straight to Chelsea's," Kate said. "I'll bring Lucky and your things over after."

"What did you have to do to make bail?" Addie asked, dreading the answer.

Kate shrugged and cast her a little smile. "I didn't have to do anything."

"Wait, what?"

"It was all Chelsea."

Addie's lips parted in surprise.

"I didn't want her to do it, certainly not the whole amount," Kate continued. "But she insisted."

"Wow," Addie said with a slow shake of her head. "I often forget she has money. She never talks about it, and she doesn't have particularly expensive taste. But she inherited a bunch from her father when he passed."

"That is quite a friend you have," Kate said.

Addie's eyes welled again, and all she could do was nod in agreement.

They drove to Chelsea's cottage north of downtown, a cute little two-bed, one-bath house with scalloped gingerbread house eaves and a white picket fence surrounding the property. A pair of Adirondack chairs, painted a cheery aqua, sat on the covered front porch. The front door was painted sunflower yellow.

Kate parked on the curb, and Chelsea pulled up behind the Subaru. Addie ran to her friend and threw her arms around her.

Unable to hold back tears, Addie took a shuddering breath. "Thank you," she whispered.

Her friend pulled back and said, "It was nothing, really. It just sits there. Besides, I'm going to get it all back just as soon as we figure out who actually killed Yuna." Chelsea's usually sunny face darkened. "And we are going to make sure they're caught and they *pay*."

Chapter Ten

IT FELT ODD IN A way to be so suddenly, completely bent on finding the killer of a woman Addie had really not known, and the little she'd known of Yuna Addie hadn't particularly liked. But it was clear she couldn't leave it up to the authorities to make sure the true murderer was caught and punished.

Kate had gone to Wild Rose to pack clothes, toiletries, and other items for Addie and then returned with two full suitcases, a sack of groceries from the fridge and pantry, and an anxious Lucky.

He bounded up the front walk to the door of the cottage, raced past Chelsea, and launched himself into Addie's arms. She buried her face in his soft fur as he wiggled around to try to lick her cheek.

"I'm so glad to see you, little boy," she murmured, kissing the top of his head before she set him on the floor.

Once everything had been moved inside and Lucky had sniffed his way through every room, the three women sat in Chelsea's cozy living room.

They ordered pizza delivery—with a separate small gluten-free pie for Chelsea—from Slice of Pie and snacked from a plate of vegetables while they waited for the pizzas. It was early afternoon and an odd time to order pizza, but it had been the first thing to come to Addie's mind when Chels asked what she wanted to eat.

Sunlight slanted through the curtains, and Addie nestled into a corner of the cushiony, blue velvet sofa. It was a comforting setting, but her nerves were frayed and her thoughts swirled anxiously.

"Have you heard from Bennett?" she asked.

"Yes, but only briefly," Kate said. "He'll check in again in a couple of hours."

"Has he made any headway with Kenneth Akido as a suspect?"

"He's working on it." Kate gave a reassuring smile, but it didn't make Addie feel much better.

If the charges against Addie weren't dropped, she'd have to return to court in a week for a pre-trial hearing. The thought of it nearly made her physically ill.

"Hey," Addie said, suddenly remembering something. "Aunt Kate, you said you might have some way to help. Something that's a little 'out there,' from the way you said it."

"Oh yes," Kate said. She looked down and reached for Lucky, who came over to her. With her gaze on the dog, she spoke haltingly. "This—well, I'm not really sure how . . ." She made a noisy sigh. "I'm just going to say it. I eat human brains now. It's the only thing that can sustain me and others like me. Our food is ethically sourced from the already-deceased only."

"Right, I knew that," Addie said, trying not to sound awkward or squirm in her seat.

"It turns out it's not like just eating a steak," Kate said. "When a Shuffler like me feeds, we get insight into the person who is the source of the food."

"Like, you can see their memories?" Chelsea asked.

"Sort of," Kate said. "It's really more than that, though. It's almost like we partially *become* them for a short time. And for that reason, we have to be really careful who we source from. A mass murderer, for example, would not be a very good source of food. Nor would someone who'd had an extremely sad or tragic life."

"Okay," Addie said, nodding. "So that's part of why you isolate yourselves during and after feeding. If you're taking on someone else's memories and personality, even just partially and temporarily, it would be safer to just chill out where nothing really bad can happen."

"Yes," Kate said. "And I had this idea. If I could somehow get access to a bit of Yuna—"

Addie gasped sharply. "You could know from her perspective what happened that led to her death?"

"Possibly," Kate said.

"But could you do that? Get a bit of Yuna's . . ." Chelsea trailed off.

"That's the sticking point," Kate said. "We have contacts in places like morgues and medical examiner offices who can, when the situation is right, get us what we need. But it's a very delicate thing. We have to treat those relationships with the utmost care, and we of course don't want to tip off any outsiders to what's up."

"You'd have to act fast, I imagine," Addie said. "I'm sure Yuna's husband and family will want to have a service soon. And if she's cremated, we're out of luck."

It was hard to think about her aunt, well, doing what she'd just described. But at the same time, Addie had a certain fascination with it all. As a kid, she'd wanted to be a doctor. But a traumatic experience where she witnessed the death of a friend's father—and felt partially responsible because her CPR hadn't saved him—had left her scared to go into the medical profession. Instead, she'd become a scientist.

"I've asked Hank to help me figure out if it would be possible," Kate said. "He should have an answer very soon."

"Is this really . . . ethical?" Addie asked.

"Well, ideally we would have the permission of the person before they were deceased, of course," Kate said. "But that's rarely possible. Our two highest priorities as a community are to do no harm to a living person and to keep our kind a secret. But to your question, we do the best we can. We have only one food source. Unfortunately, it isn't something we can grow in the ground like a head of cabbage. And so far as we know, no other species will do. Believe me, the community has looked for alternatives." She spread her hands. "This is the only way we can survive, so we try to do it as carefully and respectfully as we can."

Chelsea leaned forward, locking her gaze on Addie.

"Look, hon," Chelsea said. "It might be uncomfortable for us, but it's their way of life. And I think we need to explore every possible avenue that might keep you out of prison."

Addie nodded slowly. "You're probably right. And on that topic, I actually tried to do a tea-leaf reading. I was in the middle of it when they came to arrest me."

Kate and Chelsea both straightened with interest.

"I only got two distinct and obvious images," Addie continued. She described the dollar sign and the medical symbol and what she believed they meant. "It seems pretty obvious to me that they point to Kenneth Akido."

"Was there anything else at all?" Chels asked. "Last time you got, what, five, symbols from the reading?"

"Like I said, it got cut short. There was a picture with a bunch of tiny O's. And another with some lines and squiggles. I don't know if those two were fully drawn yet or not. There may have been more that I just didn't notice or don't remember."

"Are you comfortable telling Bennett about this?" Kate asked.

"I'm not really comfortable talking to *anyone* about it, but I'll tell him," Addie said with a shrug.

"Good." Kate leaned forward to pat Addie's hand. "Like Chelsea said, every little bit helps."

The doorbell interrupted their conversation. Kate elbowed Chelsea out of the way to get the pizza and pay the tab.

Addie looked around for her purse, which Kate had brought, but then remembered her phone and ID were at the police station. In the commotion of the bail process and the emotions of being released from jail, Addie had somehow neglected to grab the plastic bag with her personal items.

"I'll take you over there after we eat so you can get your things," Chelsea said.

"Thank you," Addie said gratefully. "You could drop me off to get my car, too, so you won't have to cart me around."

The three of them sat in the breakfast nook to eat, and in spite of her worries, Addie found she was starving. She hadn't eaten since the Subway sandwich Officer Davis had brought her the night before. The first bite of pepperoni with mushroom, the cheese gooey and almost too hot, was heaven on her tongue.

Kate had put a piece of pizza on a plate, but it was just a gesture because she didn't actually eat any. After Addie finished her first slice, Kate traded their plates, sliding the empty one in front of her with a self-conscious little smile.

Once Addie's stomach was content with a couple of pieces of pie, she sat back and drew a breath. There was something else weighing on her mind.

"Aunt Kate," she said. "I don't know how long it'll be before I can work in the shop again. But I know you can't cover full shifts yourself every day. Maybe for a few days, but you're still adjusting, and—"

Kate held up her hands. "No worries," she cut in. "You have other things to focus on, and I think I can find some extra help."

"You can?"

"There's a man in the community, Marvin, who's—well, if I'm a baby Shuffler, he's a young adult," Kate said with a little laugh. "And now that he's learned his hunger signals and cycles, he's been deemed safe to spend more time on the outside."

Addie couldn't help wondering who was making those decisions about the Shufflers. And she couldn't help worrying, too, about just how much Kate was being controlled by "the community." But Shufflers *were* dangerous if they got out of control, Addie knew that firsthand, so caution was certainly necessary. At some point, when things weren't so crazy, she'd make a point to ask Kate some deeper questions about Shuffleville and the purpose of the zombies.

"And you trust this man, Marvin?" Addie asked.

"Oh yes, he's fantastic," Kate said with bright-eyed enthusiasm. "Such a jovial, friendly man. The customers will love him."

Hm. That didn't exactly answer Addie's question like she'd hoped.

"But does he know anything about herbal medicine?" she pressed.

"A little," Kate said. "He's very eager to learn more, though. He's going to study on his own, and of course I'll be teaching him."

"Well, if you're sure," Addie said uncertainly.

She wasn't convinced it was the best idea, but Kate couldn't manage things alone yet. And it was her shop, so it was her decision.

They put away the leftovers and did a quick cleanup, and by the time they were done, Bennett had arrived.

His dark eyes were brooding and worried when he asked Addie, "Are you okay?"

She nodded. "Not the most fun night of my life, but I'm here and ready to get to work." She glanced at her aunt, who gave Addie an encouraging nod. "Before you give us your report, I think I'd better tell you about what I learned right before I was arrested."

Bennett already knew about Addie's previous brush with tasseomancy, so at least she didn't have to explain what it was or try to convince him that what she experienced was real—or as real as something that woo-woo could be.

She described the symbols in her vision.

"I hope you were able to get some info on Kenneth," Addie said. "Because it's pretty clear he's our man."

Bennett's serious expression had folded into a slight frown as she'd been speaking.

"I am working on that angle," he said. "But I don't want to shut down other avenues just yet."

It was Addie's turn to frown. "Why not? Kenneth Akido did it."

"That's entirely possible," Bennett conceded. "But I don't want to ignore any other leads."

"What other leads do you have?" Chelsea asked.

Bennett leaned forward, folding his arms on the table, and his knee lightly bumped Addie's outer thigh. The four of them were seated in the nook, and it was a cozy fit. Addie suddenly remembered her aunt telling her to say yes when Bennett asked her out. Feeling her cheeks heat slightly, she silently scolded herself for letting her thoughts wander to something so frivolous when her future was hanging in the balance.

But she couldn't help admitting to herself that he looked awfully good in a dark-heather-gray t-shirt that had pulled tighter against his muscular arms when he'd leaned forward.

Ugh, focus, Addie!

"I discovered that a while back Yuna had an affair with a doctor," Bennett said frankly. "She cut it off, but he didn't want it to end and kept pursuing her and pressuring her to leave Kenneth."

"You're thinking the doctor had something do to with it?" Addie said. "Maybe that was the medical symbol I saw?"

She chewed the inside of her cheek, suddenly doubting what a moment before she'd been so sure about.

"But why would the doctor kill Yuna?" Chelsea said. "If he really wanted to be with her, it'd make more sense for him to go after Kenneth."

"Yeah," Addie said. "And if Kenneth found out about the affair, maybe he decided to kill his wife to punish her for it. Maybe before, Kenneth was willing to go through the whole divorce proceeding, but after he found out about the affair, he was too angry."

Bennett opened his mouth to respond, but Kate spoke first.

"I'm not sure if this is going to muddy the waters, but I know something that I probably need to tell you," she said quietly. Her hand came up to the gold chain she wore, her fingers playing with it in an absent gesture. "I didn't want to betray a customer's confidence, but seeing as how Yuna is gone and Addie's in trouble . . ." She paused and took a deep breath, still seeming to hesitate.

"Does this have something to do with the tincture you created for Yuna?" Addie asked.

"It does," Kate confirmed. "It was a hormone-support formula. Yuna was trying to get pregnant."

Addie's brows pulled down. "But Kenneth was divorcing her."

Kate lifted her palms. "Maybe she thought if she got pregnant, he'd call off the divorce."

"Do you know if Yuna was against the split?" Chelsea asked, turning to Bennett. "That's one thing we really haven't talked about."

"I'm not sure about that yet," Bennett said. "But I do know Kenneth was the one filing, which indicates he was initiating the divorce."

"What else do you know about the doctor Yuna had an affair with?" Addie asked.

"Well, I know the motives aren't exactly lining up here," Bennett said. "But it turns out the doctor nearly lost his license last year."

"Do you know why?"

"He had a little drug problem, in more ways than one," Bennett said. And then he paused, and even though it wasn't like him to be dramatic, Addie almost got the idea he was hesitating for effect. She leaned in a little. "Turns out the doc was passing out scripts for fentanyl. Not only that, he's had recent struggles with addiction."

Addie's mouth dropped open in surprise.

Chapter Eleven

"DOCTOR PALBILA IS HIS NAME," Bennett continued. "From what I can gather, he really should have lost his medical license. But he agreed to enter a rehab program and he's on probation in terms of being able to write prescriptions. In many states, he wouldn't have been allowed to keep practicing."

"Let me guess," Addie said. "This doctor has friends in high places."

Bennett aimed a finger at her. "Bingo. Head of the Oregon state medical board was Palbila's advisor in med school. She's been around a long time and has a lot of sway."

Addie groaned, dropping her face into her hands. "It seems like everyone's got connections that keep them out of trouble." She looked up. "Well, not everyone. Mostly just this Doctor Palbila and also Kenneth Akido."

"Explain?" Bennett asked.

She told the story of the encounter with the police chief and his two buddies that'd happened while she was behind bars.

Her mouth twisted. "Police Chief Clemmens is Kenneth's cousin, and those other two guys are the chief's lawyer friends or whatever. They've clearly all decided that I'm going down for Yuna's murder."

"Clemmens helped to get Kenneth elected mayor," Bennett said. "The chief has been working for the past couple of years to stack the local officials with his cronies. Clemmens has his eye on bigger cities, and he'll do everything in his power to make himself look good. Rumor is he plans to make a play for the Salem Police Department. Then eventually, of course, he sees himself as Portland's Chief."

Salem was the state's capitol, but Portland was the largest city in the state. Stargaze was such a tiny town, Chief Clemmens had a lot of steps to go to make it clear to the top in Oregon.

"Sorry, but I have to go back to the lack of motive, though," Addie said. "What motive would Doctor Palbila have to kill Yuna?"

"Maybe he was actually trying to kill Kenneth," Chelsea suggested.

Addie squinted at her friend. "Hmm . . . is that possible? Did the wrong person die?"

She looked around at the others.

Bennett shook his head. "I think we need to get back to basics, here."

"Motive, means, and opportunity," Addie supplied.

He gave her a slight smile. "Exactly."

She sat back and folded her arms. "You know who gets my vote, no pun intended. Kenneth checks all three boxes."

"We don't know for sure he has fentanyl," Bennett cautioned.

"As soon as we can verify that he does, there'll be no question."

"Anybody else on your list, Bennett?" Aunt Kate asked.

"I'm still picking through the business owners Yuna was going after," he said. "It's surprisingly long."

"I'm sorry for what happened to her," Addie said, shaking her head. "But it sounds like she wasn't exactly a favorite around town."

"Truth," Chelsea agreed.

"Have you had dinner yet, Bennett?" Aunt Kate asked. "We got pizza, and I can heat some up for you if you don't mind the leftovers."

"Ah, thank you, but I should get going. I've got more to do tonight," he said, rising. Then he faced Addie. "Would you mind walking outside with me?"

Her brows shot up before she could control her expression. "Oh, uh, sure."

She led the way to the front, and he got the door for her.

Outside, the sun had set, and the late summer air was cooling pleasantly.

They walked down the two steps from the porch to the front walk, where they both stopped, and Addie faced him expectantly.

He slipped his hands into the front pockets of his dark jeans.

"I wanted to ask you something," he said. "And I hope I'm not overstepping."

Addie's pulse sped. Was he going to ask her out?

"Okay?" she prompted.

"Is your aunt okay financially?" he asked.

She blinked a couple of times. Did he want to date Kate? Wait, no, he was asking about her finances.

"I'm not hunting for any personal info," he continued. "I just want to know, if the shop had to close for a while, would she be okay?"

"Uh, I think so," Kate said. "I mean, not indefinitely, but she could probably weather a couple of weeks. Why?"

He reached up to rub at the back of his neck, and she got the sense he was worried about something that he wasn't saying.

"I hate to say it because it's so ugly, but when word gets out about your arrest, and it's already spreading as we speak, there could be . . . blowback on Wild Rose," he said.

Addie felt herself deflate as she took in what he was suggesting.

"You mean people are going to avoid Wild Rose because they'll think I poisoned Yuna's tincture?" Addie asked.

"Possibly," he said. "The details of the investigation aren't public. But this is a small town. It probably won't take much for people to put two and two together and get four, or at least what they believe is four, even if they're adding wrong." He shook his head. "I think I'm pushing this metaphor beyond its limits, but you know what I mean."

Addie closed her eyes for a moment. "I can't stand the thought of Kate losing business because of this," she whispered. "And it might not just be some money she loses out on. Her reputation . . ." She couldn't stand to carry the thought out to completion.

Bennett stepped closer to her and lightly touched her upper arm.

"Addie," he said, waiting for her to look up at him. "It's not going to come to that. It's *not*. I promise you that."

She'd been on the verge of tears, but his determination made her feel stronger.

"You can't promise that," she whispered around the lump still swelling in her throat.

"I am promising that," he said. "Just hang in there. It's going to be okay."

"Thank you, Bennett," she said. "I don't know why you're doing all this, but . . . thank you."

He'd dropped his hand, but he stood close, near enough for her to see the way he looked down into her eyes. She couldn't help feeling sure he wanted to kiss her right then, but she also knew he wouldn't do it. It wasn't the right moment.

"I'll talk to you in the morning," he said, taking a couple of steps back and keeping his eyes locked on hers. "It's going to be okay, Addie."

Then he turned, and she watched him get into his car, wave at her, and drive off.

Taking a deep breath, she told her fluttering heart to calm down and looked up at the stars.

She wanted to believe Bennett, but she was still worried that he wasn't taking Kenneth Akido seriously enough.

Addie went back inside, and her attention snagged on Kate's bloodshot eyes.

"I know you're driving again and feeling stronger," Addie said, sitting down next to her aunt. "But you're tired, and I don't want you to push yourself."

Kate ran a hand over her face and nodded. "I really should get home."

Home? Was home the shop or Shuffleville in west Stargaze?

"Are you living with Hank?" Addie asked.

"I guess you might as well know that I am," Kate said with a sheepish grin.

"He seems like a good man, one who wants to take care of you."

"Part of that is my new, uh, status, but yes, he is a good man."

"I'm so happy for you," Addie said, beaming with genuine joy. "You've spent a lot of years on your own, which is fine if that's what you wanted, but this . . . new life actually seems to suit you."

Kate tilted her head, sending her gaze up to a corner of the room, and her eyes grew thoughtful. "You know, it probably seems strange, but it does suit me. I love being part of the community. I love being with Hank." She focused on Addie. "But I miss the shop, and you, and I *really* miss my magic."

Addie patted her aunt's knee. "You need to get home."

Kate straightened. "I really do."

She stood just as Chelsea came in with a pile of bedding in her arms.

"Do you have to go?" she asked Kate.

"Before I turn into a pumpkin," Kate said, grabbing her purse and scooting to the door. She blew kisses to Addie and Chelsea. "Get some sleep. You've both earned it. We'll talk in the morning. Oh, and Addie, Maureen will want to meet with you. I told her nine was okay, I hope that works. She'll come here."

"Oh," Addie said. She'd been riding on the wave of Bennett's commitment to clearing her and the comfort of people who cared about her. But the mention of the lawyer brought Addie crashing back down. She forced a smile. "That's fine. Thank you so much for finding her and setting it all up."

Aunt Kate left, and Addie tried not to feel forlorn about her aunt's departure.

"I found some sheets and blankets," Chelsea said. "Why don't we make up the spare bed so it's ready when you want to crash?"

Addie followed her into the second bedroom, which had a cute little antique rolltop desk, white linen curtains, and walls painted the faded gray violet of dried lavender buds. Chelsea had lit a green candle on the dresser, and the room had a pleasant herbal floral smell.

Together, they put the sheets and blankets on the bed and then went back to the living room, where Chelsea dimmed the lights and lit another candle that sat on the coffee table.

"If you're tired, we can turn in," she said.

Addie shook her head. "I am tired, but I don't think I can go to sleep yet."

Chelsea pulled her feet up, curling into the corner of the sofa and reaching for a pillow, which she wrapped her arms around.

"Everything has suddenly become about me. How are *you* doing?" Addie asked.

"Oh, I'm fine," Chelsea said with a little laugh.

"No really, what's going on with you? Just tell me about normal things. Everyday life that doesn't involve poison or murder or lawyers or jail. Pretty please?"

Chelsea tipped her head back in amusement. "Well, okay. Things are good at the boutique. Business is steady."

"What about your own creations?" Addie asked. "Have you started designing?"

She knew Chelsea loved fashion, but it ran deeper than that. She loved fabrics, colors, and textures in a way that went beyond most people's interest in clothes. It was her dream to design and make her own clothing line.

"I've been making sketches for years," Chelsea said. She gestured to a card table on which sat a sewing machine. "But I'm not that great at sewing yet."

There were stacks of fabric on the floor under the table. And next to it was a stand that looked like a cloth-covered torso. A swath of silky-looking pale-pink fabric was draped around it.

"Making progress?" Addie asked.

"Not as fast as I'd like," Chelsea said ruefully. Then her eyes sparkled. "But it's so much fun!"

"Well, when you're ready to show off what you've made, I'd love to see it."

You know, if I'm not in prison for murder.

"So, what did Bennett say outside?" Chelsea tilted her head in curiosity. She gave a sly smile. "Or is it private?" she asked in a singsong voice.

"Oh, it's not really private." Addie looked down and pulled at a frayed thread at the edge of a small hole forming on the knee of her jeans. "He wanted to warn me that Wild Rose could be adversely affected by all of this."

Chelsea let out a soft breath, her mood sobering. "That would be terrible."

"I know," Addie said. "It's just another reason we've *got* to figure out who killed Yuna."

"You know what? I think we're going to have a breakthrough tomorrow."

"What makes you so sure?" Addie asked.

"Just a feeling," Chelsea said with a firm nod.

Was Chelsea reading auras again? Did she have some intuitive hit about the case?

Either way, Addie appreciated her friend's optimism but wasn't sure she shared it. No matter what, Chelsea was right: the next day they sorely needed to make some headway.

Chapter Twelve

MAUREEN KAPOSKY ARRIVED AT TWO minutes before nine the next morning, leather satchel in one hand and large to-go coffee in the other.

She sat down with Addie in Chelsea's cheery living room. Chelsea had already left to open her boutique, and Addie couldn't help feeling a little forlorn at having to deal with legal stuff alone.

"You haven't been back to your aunt's shop, have you?" Maureen asked.

"No, of course not," Addie said.

"Good. Let's keep it that way."

Addie suppressed a frown at the lawyer's clipped tone.

Maureen pulled out a yellow pad and flipped to a blank page.

"Okay, why don't you tell me everything about your interactions with Yuna Akido," she said.

Addie spoke while Maureen made notes and peppered in questions.

"And Kenneth Akido?" Maureen asked.

"Never met him or talked to him before the night Yuna died," Addie said. She straightened and folded her hands. "I believe he killed his wife. He's got motive, and—"

Maureen held up her hand palm out with her pen balanced between her thumb and finger.

"Nope, I'm going to stop you right there," she said. "This isn't like on TV. Lawyers aren't detectives. I'm not going to run out and question other suspects or look for evidence."

"Don't you want to be able to offer an alternate theory for who killed Yuna?" Addie asked, her brows pulling in.

"It's best if we just stick to what we know and concentrate on shooting down whatever the prosecution comes up with."

"But if there's a strong case for someone else having committed the crime, that *would* help us shoot down the charge against me," Addie argued.

"Like I said, we're not here to play detective," Maureen said, looking over the tops of her readers at Addie. "Once we know the details of the prosecution's evidence against you, we'll focus all our efforts on picking it apart. That may or may not include offering up alternative suspects."

Addie's mouth hardened as she tried to tamp down her annoyance. She scrutinized her lawyer. Maureen Kaposky wasn't in someone's pocket, was she?

"Did you know Yuna?" Addie blurted out.

"I knew who she was," Maureen said, glancing up.

"What about Kenneth Akido, Police Chief Clemmens, or a Doctor Palbila?"

Maureen lowered her chin, shooting a piercing gaze at Addie. "No. Ms. James, despite the fact that many in my line of work aren't above board, I've made it my professional mission to be impeccable in my integrity and ethics. Ask around if you need to. You may not find me fun or friendly, but I'm not here for those things. I'm here to represent you better than anyone else in this town could. Am I clear?"

"You're clear," Addie said, trying to release her fears.

And that was all they were, she realized—paranoid fears. When she took a slow breath and focused on her gut feelings, she knew her thoughts had started to spin out of control. Maureen Kaposky wasn't there to be Addie's BFF. Maureen was there to fight like heck on Addie's behalf, and she had to let Maureen do her job.

"How about you leave the questions to me? I do charge by the hour, you know," Maureen said.

After another forty-five minutes, Addie's temples throbbed with the beginnings of a headache. When Maureen gathered up her things, Addie was more than happy to show her to the door.

The lawyer stepped outside and then turned to Addie.

"I want to be straight with you, Addie," Maureen said. "You need to keep a low profile. Nosing around is only going to hurt your case. Don't play detective." She didn't wait for Addie's answer.

By the time Maureen drove away, Addie was frazzled and irritated. The lawyer hadn't wanted to talk about things that Addie thought were pretty darn important—like Kenneth Akido and his desire to divorce his wife without losing his family money—and she wasn't a huge fan of Maureen's terse, dismissive manner.

As Maureen had said, she was a lawyer, not an investigator. But if Addie could come up with a lead on another suspect that was rock solid, Maureen wouldn't be able to ignore it.

Addie went back inside, where she toasted a bagel and then slathered it with cream cheese. She texted Bennett, asking what he was up to. A few minutes later, he messaged back saying he was following some leads and would catch up with her midday.

She started in on the second half of her bagel and was surprised to see a message from Trey Parkinson, who owned the guitar shop next to Wild Rose Teas and Apothecary. Well, it *would* be a guitar shop once he finished renovating the inside.

Hi Addie, I just saw your aunt and she told me you've run into some trouble. If you're in the mood to blow off some steam later, hit me up. I'm free after 4:30.

Run into some trouble?

That was one way to put it.

A small smile touched her lips at the thought of Trey's gray-green eyes framed by those long, dark lashes. He was nice. Friendly. And definitely cute.

But she didn't exactly have the luxury of going on hikes or grabbing a bite. Or did she? Maybe it would do her good to do something normal. Besides, if Bennett or Maureen or the police or anyone else had something urgent, they all knew how to get a hold of her.

She scooped up her phone and texted back.

That would be great. If you don't mind hanging out with a suspected criminal, that is. Oh, and I need to stay in the city limits for reasons that are painfully obvious.

A few seconds later he replied.

I can take the heat. Besides, I know you're innocent. How about 5:30?

Five thirty. Did that mean dinner? Was this officially a date?

Addie shrugged. Whether it was a date or not, she was game. She liked Trey. He didn't have Bennett's air of mystery and seriousness, but Trey was a singer who played guitar and wrote his own songs, and even his speaking voice had a soulful rasp to it. He was attractive and interesting, and why not?

Sure, she texted back. *I'll meet you at Style, Chelsea's boutique.*

The clothing store was far enough away from Wild Rose that no one could accuse Addie of lurking around her aunt's shop.

Her phone rang, and the caller ID showed it was Kate.

"Addie, we're going to get it," Kate said, excitement clear in her voice.

"Get what?"

"Our *connection* with the *morgue* came through."

Addie sucked in a breath and pressed her free hand into her stomach.

"Really?" she said. "You're going to get a piece of Yuna's . . . you know?"

"Yes," Kate said. "And I think you should witness it."

Addie cringed. "Uh, I don't know about that."

"It'll be okay," Kate said. "You don't have to watch the actual consumption. But you should be there to hear whatever comes out of my mouth afterward."

"If you're sure," Addie said doubtfully.

"I am."

"When?"

"Twenty minutes. You'll need to come to Shuffleville, though. I can send you the address."

"But what about the shop?" Addie asked.

"I'll have Marvin cover," Kate said. "He can work the register and fill tea orders. If someone needs a tincture and he's not comfortable doing that, I'll have him tell them to come back later."

"Okay," Addie said. "Text me where to meet you."

"Will do, see you soon."

Addie ended the call and popped the last of her bagel in her mouth, trying not to think about what her aunt was about to do. She dumped her plate and glass in the dishwasher and then went to let Lucky out into the back yard.

Kate sent the address, and Addie called Lucky inside after a few minutes.

She grabbed her keys and purse, locked up with the spare key Chelsea had left, and headed out for west Stargaze and Shuffleville.

Driving downtown and then continuing on, Addie couldn't help noticing how the surroundings changed the farther west she went.

It went from business plazas and government buildings to the heart of downtown with people and cars moving busily, to the west edge of downtown where Wild Rose was located, to an area where few people were walking around.

There were warehouses, self-storage units, and truck lots.

She passed Bowl of Plenty, a soup kitchen where Aunt Kate volunteered.

And then the buildings shifted from industrial to residential. But the apartment complexes weren't modern or pretty. There was a quietness to the area that was vaguely unsettling, and warning signs that read "Keep Out After Dark" only added a whisper of foreboding that pinged at the back of her mind.

Unlike last time she'd been in west Stargaze, she knew why there were ominous signs. But Aunt Kate wouldn't have asked Addie to come if it were a dangerous time to do so. Plus, this was her aunt's home now.

Addie checked the GPS again. The apartment she was looking for was in the tallest complex. Taking a left past a tired-looking playground with outdated equipment, she started looking for parking. She pulled into a spot on the curb and then called Kate.

"Hi, I'm here," she said. "Just across the street from the building's main entrance, I think."

"Great, I'll come to get you," Aunt Kate said.

Addie decided to stay in her car until she her aunt appeared. It wasn't that she saw any particular risk, but the memory of being surrounded by a shuffling, glassy-eyed crowd quickly closing in on her still made her shiver. At the time, she hadn't known she'd stumbled into the zombie community, and it could have ended badly.

The complex door swung open, and Kate waved.

Addie hopped out and hurried across the street.

"Welcome to Shuffleville," Kate said, holding the door until Addie was inside the lobby.

There was a pair of elevator doors, a fire door leading to the staircase, and a bank of mailboxes filling a wall. Those were really the only features. There wasn't even a plant or a framed piece of art to warm up the space.

"Are you sure it's okay that I'm here?" Addie asked in a low voice.

"Oh yes," Kate said. "We're all fed and happy for the time being."

She went to the elevator and punched the up arrow.

Addie couldn't help comparing the somewhat dingy lobby to Kate's comfortable apartment above Wild Rose.

"It's kind of . . . sparse, isn't it?" Addie asked, rubbing her hands up and down her upper arms. She wasn't sure if it was really chilly in the building, or if she just had nervous shivers.

"It is," Kate said. "But by consensus of the community, we keep things as simple as possible."

The elevator doors opened, and a man in his early 30s, wearing a Hawaiian shirt, cargo shorts, and flipflops, got off.

"Hi, Kate," he said with an easy smile. "How are you?"

"Doing well, thanks," she said, returning his smile. But she didn't introduce the man to Addie, instead hopping onto the elevator.

Addie scooted after her aunt.

"Don't worry," Kate said, poking the button for the eighth floor. "That wasn't poor manners. We don't do introductions between Shufflers and outsiders unless absolutely necessary. We want to limit time of contact."

"Does that have something to do with exposing my, uh, scent?" Addie asked.

Bennett had explained a little about Shufflers when he'd saved her from the zombie horde she'd stumbled into. He'd been initially very worried the newer, less disciplined Shufflers would pick up her scent trail and try to follow her home.

"Exactly," Kate said with a nod.

She didn't seem particularly concerned, so Addie tried to relax.

When the elevator stopped, Addie followed her aunt to the door marked 813.

"Come on in," Kate invited.

Addie was relieved to see that the apartment appeared to be a little more in line with Kate's style, with a blue-and-white plaid sofa set up facing a TV, some framed nature photos on the walls, an overstuffed armchair with a cheery floral pillow, crisp white curtains, and a handmade colorful knit throw draped across the back of the sofa.

The space was small, though, with a kitchen sharing the living space.

Addie recognized Hank's head, bent so he could peer into the fridge.

He straightened and turned around, giving her a smile.

"Hello, there, Addie," he said and lifted the plastic storage container he'd pulled from the fridge. "This is the stuff. Fingers crossed it'll help your case."

Addie forced a smile as her gaze snagged on the plastic container. Was there really a chunk of Yuna's *brain* in there? She tried not to grimace.

"Hi, Hank. I really do appreciate this, and I hope it didn't cause any trouble."

"We had to pull some strings, but hopefully it'll be worth it."

All Addie could do was nod.

Kate, on the other hand, seemed quite eager. She went to stand next to Hank, his broad shoulders and towering form making her look small, so she could peer into the container when he pulled off the lid.

"Let's do this," she said, rubbing her hands together. She looked up at Addie. "Want to take a look?"

Addie went to stand on the other side of the kitchen's peninsula counter, keeping it between her and the couple.

"Normally, I'd probably say yes out of intellectual curiosity," Addie said. "But if you don't mind, I'll decline."

"Totally understandable," Hank said.

When Aunt Kate produced a knife and fork and took them and the container to the table where she sat down, Addie studiously looked off to the side. She knew what was happening, but she didn't want to watch it. Focusing on taking even breaths and ignoring her churning stomach, Addie did her best to keep a neutral expression. She nearly faltered when she heard her aunt make a low hum of satisfaction and knew she'd taken a bite.

"How long until—" Addie started to ask.

But Kate's keening moan cut Addie off. Her gaze whipped to her aunt, and she took a step back.

Aunt Kate's eyes were rolling around, and she was swaying. She tipped her head back, her mouth hanging open. Addie looked at Hank in alarm.

"It's okay. This is normal," Hank whispered. Then he turned to Kate, and in a normal voice said, "Yuna?"

Kate stopped swaying and moaning, leveled her chin, and stared into space.

Hank gave her a moment before saying, "Yuna, let's remember what happened right before you died."

Kate's eyelids fluttered for a moment, and then she lifted her hands and focused her gaze.

"Oh, *this* one," Kate murmured. She had her hands up and seemed to be miming the action of scrolling on a phone. "Aren't you a beauty? Hm, full price. Hey, life's too short to wait for a sale."

Addie's brows rose.

Kate looked up suddenly, peering past Addie as if she wasn't there.

Aunt Kate's face hardened. "Did you refill your migraine meds?" A pause. Then a scoff. "So what? I have a headache. Where's the bottle?"

She set her imaginary phone down on her lap and acted out twisting a cap off a bottle.

"These things are *weak*. A few pills will do the trick," she said. She lifted her hand to her mouth and then made a swallowing motion. Looking up and to the side, she nodded. "I'm glad Lisette decided to start serving dinner. There's literally no fine dining in this dinky town. God, I can hardly wait for a glass of wine."

As Addie watched, Kate appeared to step out of a car, turn, and slam the door.

"Would it kill you to look like you're happy to have dinner with your wife?" she asked and then set off walking across the room.

When Kate reached the sofa, she stopped. Then she began swaying again.

"Is she done?" Addie whispered after a few seconds.

"Looks like it," Hank whispered back.

He went over to Kate and led her to the sofa, where she curled up on her side. He pulled the blanket over her.

Addie's eyes met Hank's.

Her heart was pounding, and she was nearly breathless. What she'd just witnessed, if she understood correctly, proved what she'd suspected. Kenneth Akido had given his wife some pills, and those pills had killed her minutes later.

"That had to be a reenactment of Yuna and her husband driving to dinner at La Petite Patisserie, right?" Addie asked.

"Without a doubt," Hank said, his face grave.

Addie wished Kate were awake so they could talk about what had just happened. It wasn't the kind of evidence that could be presented to the police, but it backed up what Addie already knew. Kenneth Akido was the murderer.

"How long until Kate wakes up?" Addie asked.

"It'll be several hours," Hank said. "I'd invite you to stay and wait, but we like to keep outsiders here for as little time as possible. It's for your own safety."

"Right, of course," Addie said absently.

"I'll walk you down," he said. "Your aunt will be fine alone for a few minutes. She's not going anywhere."

Hank escorted Addie to her car, and once she was inside with the doors locked, she pulled out her phone, intending to call Chelsea.

But before she could, it rang with Bennett's name popping up on the screen.

"Hello?"

"Addie, things just took a turn," Bennett said. He sounded a little out of breath.

She gripped her phone harder. "What happened?"

"Kenneth Akido is dead."

Chapter Thirteen

ADDIE BLINKED, WONDERING IF SHE'D heard Bennett correctly.

"Did you just say Kenneth Akido is dead?" she asked.

"Yes," Bennett confirmed. "The news hasn't been released to the public yet, but I've got a connection in the police department."

Addie squinted into the distance. "How did he die?"

"He was attacked in his home very early this morning," Bennett said.

"That's unfortunate, and not just for him," Addie said. "Bennett, Kenneth killed Yuna. I've got proof. Well, not the *normal* kind of proof, but it's close enough."

"Explain?"

Addie told him about what Aunt Kate had acted out after taking a bite of Yuna's brain.

"I'm almost certain Kenneth didn't do it," Bennett said.

Addie frowned. "Just because he's dead doesn't mean he's innocent."

"No, there's more," he said. "Apparently the killer rifled through the bathroom. In particular, the medicine cabinet."

"Okay?" Addie tilted her head, not quite seeing where he was headed.

"And there's video of the killer coming and going, caught by the Akido's home security system. They've got one of those doorbell cameras. The guy was wearing a mask, but he left with a fistful of prescription bottles."

"I still don't see why that clears Kenneth," Addie said. "In Kate's vision, or whatever it was, Kenneth gave Yuna his pills. He must have replaced his headache medicine with fentanyl and then just had to wait until she asked for some. She'd clearly used his meds before."

"I don't think that's the scenario we're dealing with here," Bennett said.

"Then what do you think happened?" Addie asked, trying not to get irritable.

Seriously, why was Bennett so resistant to her theory?

"I think that doctor, Palbila, the one Yuna had an affair with, tried to off Kenneth."

"Eh, that seems like a much bigger stretch."

"Maybe on the surface, but hear me out," Bennett said. "Here's the kicker. Kenneth was *going* to Doctor Palbila."

"Wait, you're saying Palbila prescribed those meds to Kenneth?"

"I am. And I'd thought Kenneth knew about the affair, but he never found out about it."

"And you said the doc didn't want to break it off with Yuna," Addie said.

"Yes, and she was trying to get pregnant with her husband," Bennett said. "I think she'd decided to commit to the marriage in earnest."

"Are you sure Kenneth didn't know about the affair, though?" Addie asked. "I mean, he filed for divorce."

"They'd been having problems for years," Bennett said. "In fact, Kenneth had talked to a divorce attorney two years prior but then decided not to file."

Addie slumped as her thoughts whirled.

"So, you think the doc intended to off Kenneth so Yuna would finally be with him," she said.

"And then, after Yuna took the pills and died, Doctor Palbila needed to remove the fentanyl so no one could trace the killing back to his prescription."

Her face scrunched in consternation, and she shook her head. "I don't know, part of it doesn't quite fit together for me."

"How so?" Bennett asked, and he seemed genuinely interested in hearing her answer.

"Well, for one thing, wouldn't Kenneth have noticed what was on the prescription label?" she mused. "He took several prescriptions, and the bottles I saw in his bag were all the same size. He'd have to at least glance at the label to make sure he'd grabbed the right one. Also, when you start a new prescription, the pharmacist always asks if you have questions or want a consult. Someone at the pharmacy would have asked him if he'd used fentanyl before. And don't you have to show ID and get logged in a system when you get an opioid prescription?"

"Hm," Bennett murmured. "You're right, something doesn't quite fit. I think we need to back up a sec. We've both been assuming that the fentanyl isn't Kenneth's normal migraine medicine, that someone replaced the normal drug with this far more dangerous one."

"True," Addie agreed. "Are you thinking that's an incorrect assumption?"

"It could be," he said. "So, let's look at that. If Kenneth's headache drug has always been fentanyl, and according to Kate's vision Yuna had taken it before, it shouldn't have killed her the other night."

"I agree," Addie said. "But if we assume that fentanyl *wasn't* Kenneth's normal headache medicine, then how did he come by it and why?"

"And we're back to the doctor. Maybe."

"Or . . ." Addie said. "Kenneth could have gotten it on the black market, dumped out his usual headache pills, and replaced them with fentanyl."

"If he were really bent on killing her, that's a possibility," Bennett conceded.

"Which way are you leaning? What does your gut say?"

There was a pause. "That it wasn't Kenneth," he said finally. "Honestly, Addie, I wish I thought it *was* Kenneth. That would make this all a lot simpler. What does your gut say?"

She gave a short, rueful laugh. "Oh, you know I'm not great at listening to my instincts. But I'm more torn than I was before you called me. I was so sure it was Kenneth, but the doctor has motive and possibly means, too." Blowing out a long breath, she pushed her hair off her forehead. "I'm not tossing Kenneth out, but I'll admit the doctor could have done it. I don't know, my sense is neither of them fit perfectly."

"Hey, that's your instincts talking," Bennett said, his tone warming. She imagined him with a slight smile on his lips. "You're better at that part than you think you are."

"Well, there's obviously more to the story," she said. "I think . . . I think I'm going to try the tea-leaf reading again. Maybe it'll give us a nudge one way or the other."

"Might as well," he said. "I'm going to circle back with my contact at the police department, and I'll update you in a few hours."

"Okay, thanks, Bennett."

"Of course."

Addie hung up, started her car, and drove back to Chelsea's deep in thought. The entire drive, Addie ping-ponged back and forth between Kenneth and Doctor Palbila.

It'd be really grand if the police managed to catch Kenneth's attacker, because if it turned out to be the doctor, that would solidify him as Yuna's killer. Though according to Bennett's theory, Yuna's death was an accidental killing.

At Chelsea's cottage, Addie let Lucky out and sat down on one of the lawn chairs while he sniffed the flower beds and did his business.

Back inside, she found a mug and small plate, which would have to do in place of a proper cup and saucer. With the mug full of water and heating in the microwave, she searched the pantry until she found a box of mint, ginger, and lemon tea bags.

Needing loose tea for the tasseomancy reading, she used a kitchen knife to cut open two bags. She dumped the contents into the hot water and stirred them around with a spoon.

Sitting in the breakfast nook, she peered down into the mug and thought about the case. She focused on Yuna's death as she sipped the tea, and when she got down to the dregs, she swirled the mug and then turned it over onto the plate.

With the cup turned up again, she examined the patterns left by the residual tea clinging to the sides and bottom.

Her insides began to swim and buzz, and a swishing noise filled her ears.

Leaning forward, she stared with unblinking intensity into the mug as lines formed to delineate little symbols.

There was the medical symbol with the two snakes, likely related to the pills Yuna had taken.

The dollar sign, indicating money was involved somehow.

The little circles. She counted twelve of them in three neat rows. Eggs? Bubbles? She wasn't sure.

And a fourth symbol with squiggles and lines.

Addie squinted, waiting for more detail to form. It looked like . . . two figures. A taller one with short hair and a triangle torso with the broad part at the top, most likely a man. And a shorter one with squiggly lines showing long wavy hair and an hourglass torso—a woman, Addie guessed. The two little stick figures were holding hands—no, not quite. Their hands reached toward each other, but there was a jagged line between them.

A fracture in a relationship. A split, a divorce perhaps?

The swishing was starting to sound like words—a whisper.

Addie turned her focus to the sound.

Love money, love money, love money . . .

The two words continued to repeat for half a minute or so and then faded into silence. The symbols in the tea leaves were gone, too.

Addie sat back and pressed the heels of her palms against her closed eyelids.

"Love and money," she murmured.

Dropping her hands to the table, she stared out the window, her eyes unfocused.

The hints could point to Kenneth Akido as the one who killed Yuna.

Or they could be indicating Doctor Palbila. Maybe. Certainly the love part.

But the money part? The connection to Kenneth seemed clearer there. He'd been worried about losing money when he divorced Yuna. As far as Addie knew, though, money wasn't really a factor in the affair between Yuna and the doctor.

Addie let out a noisy, frustrated breath and leaned over the mug.

"Why can't you just *tell* me?" she hollered into it.

She stood and rinsed the tea out in the sink, thinking about the symbols in the leaves.

The split between the man and woman was fairly clear—a rift in a relationship.

But the little circles were still a mystery.

Restless, she emptied the clean dishes from the dishwasher, swept the patio in the back yard, and then took Lucky around the block.

When Chelsea's yellow bug pulled up, Addie was thrilled to have someone to talk to.

She told Chelsea about Kate's vision and then drew out the symbols in the tea leaves and repeated the whispered words. Addie also recounted how she and Bennett had gone back and forth between Kenneth and the doctor as the murder suspects.

"News about Kenneth is starting to make the rounds," Chelsea said. "I overheard some people talking about it when I went to the post office."

"What do you think?" Addie asked. "Kenneth or Palbila?"

Chelsea frowned and looked off to the side, a thoughtful expression on her face.

"It's a tough one," she said. "From what you've told me, I'd be leaning toward Kenneth for the reasons you are, too."

"But . . . ?" Addie prompted when Chelsea seemed to hesitate.

"I'm just not totally convinced it was Kenneth, even if logic seems to be pointing to him."

"Is this your intuition speaking or something more?" Addie asked.

"Something more. When we were at La Petite Patisserie that night, I saw Kenneth and Yuna. I mean, they weren't there very long before Yuna collapsed, but in the look I got, I saw their . . ."

"Auras. Right?"

Chelsea nodded. "And I distinctly remember Kenneth's. It was perturbed, like he was very stressed, but it didn't seem like the aura of a man who'd just handed his wife pills that he intended to end her life with. It was light, for the most part. People who harm others or have bad intentions don't have that much lightness in their auras. Kenneth's was in the normal range."

Addie nodded, not quite trusting herself to respond. Her first instinct was to throw up her hands and argue that auras didn't actually *mean* anything. But she couldn't very well do that when she'd just finished talking seriously about little pictures she'd seen in soggy tea leaves.

"Okayyy," Addie said slowly. "Did you happen to see anything in Yuna's aura?"

Chelsea shook her head. "Nothing out of the ordinary."

Addie shrugged. "Not that it probably would have helped us, but I was just curious."

She really was trying to be more open-minded. It probably helped that her own freedom was on the line. She'd take anything that might help.

"How often do you see someone with a, uh, dark aura?" Addie asked.

"Not that often, I guess. But it's a spectrum of lightness and darkness."

"So, someone has to have done something really bad to have that dark aura?"

"Well, I don't know that for sure," Chelsea said. "Because in most cases I don't know the person, so I don't know the cause of their aura quality."

"But I take it you've known enough of them personally to confirm that a certain type of aura corresponds to . . . bad things."

"I think I can say that, yeah. And it's not like a dark aura is *always* dark, necessarily. Maybe with some people it's that way, but others have dark and light times, I guess. Most of us have dark-ish moments, right? But some people have a lot of darkness in them, and it rarely leaves."

Addie watched Chelsea's face as she spoke. Even though Chelsea had grown up with money and for the most part had been well-liked in school, her childhood had been sad. She'd lost her mother young, and her father had been cold and controlling and, from what Addie could gather, abusively so. He'd never physically harmed Chelsea, as far as Addie knew, but Chelsea had feared her father even as she'd tried in her childlike ways to forge some warmth in their relationship.

In the summers Addie had spent in Stargaze running around with Chelsea, they'd mostly avoided going to her home, instead choosing to hang out with Aunt Kate at Wild Rose, swimming in Jade Lake, and camping out.

What little Addie had known of Chelsea's father had made her want to spend as little time as possible in his house, too.

Addie suspected that Chelsea was remembering her father's aura when she spoke of dark moments.

"Chelsea." Addie leaned forward. "I have an idea."

"What's that?"

"You could make an appointment to see Doctor Palbila. I'd really like to hear what *his* aura looks like."

Chapter Fourteen

CHELSEA MANAGED TO SET AN appointment with Doctor Palbila for the next day. She was lucky there'd been a cancellation just that morning.

After that, they'd made a list of everything they knew so far about the murder. All the clues, including Kate's vision, Addie's tasseomancy reading, and Chelsea's aura description of Kenneth Akido.

By the time they'd finished, they'd filled an entire page in Chelsea's notebook, but they were still no more certain about who the murderer was.

Addie checked the time on her phone and sat up straight on the sofa.

"Oh! I need to get ready," she said.

"Ready for what?" Chelsea asked, capping her purple gel pen.

"I'm meeting Trey soon," Addie said. "He offered to meet up to give me a break from everything." She held up a hand. "Not that I need a break from *you*, of course."

Chelsea shook her head with a little smile. "No offense taken. You do need to get out. Only . . ."

"What?"

"Well, I'm surprised you're taking that break with Trey." She tapped her lower lip with the end of her pen. "You do know this is a date, right?"

Addie shrugged. "Not really. It's not that . . . formal. Besides, who else would I be taking a break with?"

She asked it innocently enough, but she knew very well that Chelsea was thinking of Bennett. The thing was, Addie liked Bennett. A lot. But she wasn't positive that he was interested in her. Not enough, anyway. Sure, he was being very generous about helping her out, but he and Kate had known each other for years. He'd started out as a customer who came in for a custom tincture, but they'd ended up becoming friends. So Addie knew he was offering his services because of Kate, too.

"Oh, maybe some tall, dark, and handsome type," Chelsea said playfully.

Addie looked around with comical exaggeration. "Well, I don't see any of those types asking me out, so . . ."

"You could ask him out."

"Eh, I don't think I'm up for the pursuit yet," Addie said, shaking her head. "It's literally only been a couple months since I left Jeremy."

Since she "left" Jeremy?

More like since she fled San Francisco sobbing after discovering her dirtbag fiancé cheating on her. But hey, a girl could reframe things in retrospect. That was allowed, right?

"True," Chelsea said. "No need to be in a rush."

"Exactly."

Addie went into her bedroom to change into a denim skirt and a crossover sleeveless top with a crisp navy stripe pattern on it. She put on a little more mascara, spritzed on some herby-floral body spray, and stepped into brown leather sandals with a flat heel. She wanted to keep it casual, and if they ended up walking around, she didn't want to be wearing torture devices on her feet.

"You look niiice," Chelsea crooned when Addie went back out into the living room.

Addie rolled her eyes. "Not a date."

"Sure, sure."

"Have fun," Chelsea called as Addie slung her purse across her chest and made for the door.

"Thanks, Chels. See you in a while."

Addie was looking forward to seeing Trey, but she couldn't help wondering if she should really be doing this. She was out on bail, formally accused of *killing someone*, for goodness' sake.

She took a deep breath, trying to calm down as she steered through Chelsea's neighborhood toward downtown. Finding a place to park at the end of the block where Chelsea's boutique was located, Addie shifted into park and shut off the engine.

Trey pulled up across the street and leaned over to wave at her through his passenger window. She grinned and waved back.

He came across to meet her, and she couldn't help taking in his easy style—jeans slightly worn, a short-sleeved button down from a well-known outdoor apparel company, and black Vans. The green stripes in his shirt brought out the green flecks in his hazel-gray eyes.

"How's the life of the criminal?" he asked in his slightly raspy, rich voice.

"Oh, you know, I'm pretty exhausted from dodging the law," she said with a little grin.

"Anything in particular you'd like to do?" he asked.

"I wouldn't mind stretching my legs a little. How about if we walk around, and if we see a good place to eat, we could grab a bite?"

"Sounds good."

She pointed. "Let's go this way, away from Wild Rose, if you don't mind. I don't want to accidentally wander over there."

"Right," he said. "We don't want to make trouble."

The way he said the word trouble, looking at her from under his brows with a sparkle in his eyes, gave her a tiny, delightful shiver.

As they walked, she asked him how the work on his store was coming along. He planned to sell guitars and offer lessons. And he was building a stage in the back corner so the store could also serve as a small venue for live performances. Addie knew he wrote his own songs and could sing and play, but she'd never heard him. She'd like to, though, she realized. Maybe once the legal stuff blew over . . .

She suppressed a sigh.

Nothing was going to blow over if another suspect wasn't identified.

"Hey, everything okay?" Trey asked, bending to look into her eyes. "I mean, I know it's not okay, but . . . do you want to talk about it?"

"No. Maybe." Addie gave a humorless laugh. "I don't know."

"I can't imagine how scary this must be," he said.

"It just seems like a bad dream. I could never *poison* someone," she said. She happened to look up at the couple they were passing and noticed their stares. "But there's an actual, real chance I could take the blame for this."

She stopped talking abruptly.

Scanning the sidewalk and looking across the street, she noticed eyes on her, and she wanted to shrink.

"What's wrong?" Trey asked and cast her a sharp look.

"People are staring at me," she said in a low voice. "They're looking at me like—like I'm a killer."

He followed her gaze. Then he pointed down a side street. "Let's go that way. It's less busy." He waited half a block before adding, "And for the record, I don't think they were looking at you like you were a killer."

He guided her over to a bench, where they sat down.

"Maybe you're right," Addie said. "But there are people in this town who truly do want to see me go to prison."

"Like who?"

She shook her head, not wanting to talk about Police Chief Clemmens and his buddies. "It's better if I don't get into it. I just . . . it's hard to believe this is my life, you know?"

"Hey, it's your life right now. But this is going to get sorted out."

She nodded, suddenly too downtrodden to even express gratitude for the comfort he was offering.

"Sorry I'm such a wet blanket," she said ruefully.

"No need to apologize," he said. "I asked you out knowing you were really going through it and not expecting you to be in high spirits."

I asked you out.

Maybe he did see it as a date. Either way, he was being kind and patient.

"Are you hungry?" she asked.

He shrugged a shoulder and gave her a small smile. "I am if you are."

She looked around to see what was nearby, and her gaze fell on a store across the street.

"Oh, I didn't realize we were here," she said, partly to herself.

"Where?" he asked, also looking across the street.

"That's Glazed, the donut shop."

"Hey, I'm up for donuts for dinner if that sounds good."

She shook her head and cast him a faint smile. "No, that's not what I was thinking, although I've never been one to turn a good donut down." Standing, she smoothed her skirt. "I think I would like to walk by there, though."

Something was prickling at the back of her mind.

"Sure," he said.

They went down to the corner, crossed the street, and then Addie touched Trey's arm and stopped.

Leaning in, she spoke at a whisper, even though no one else was near.

"Just so you don't think I'm totally crazy, I should tell you that Edna, one of the owners of Glazed"—she nodded at the donut store—"had been really upset with Yuna. Edna actually spoke in terms that could, in retrospect, seem threatening." Addie paused, pulling her brows down in a slight frown. "I wasn't really considering Edna as a suspect, because there are two other people who seemed more obvious, but . . ."

"You've got a hunch?" Trey asked after a few seconds passed and Addie didn't finish her sentence.

She nodded. "I don't even know what it is, but there's this little . . . *nudge* at the back of my mind. Like there's something I need to remember but can't quite."

"Let's stroll past," he said. "Maybe it'll surface."

She slowed as they got to the window of Glazed and then stopped to look in.

There was a table showing a display of cake stands stacked with donuts—strawberry, chocolate, lemon, vanilla frosted, maple bars, and a variety of donuts decorated with sprinkles and colored sugar crystals.

An open box showed twelve cake donuts with a sign that said, "Save $2 when you buy a dozen!" in a whimsical, curling font.

The walls of the shop were painted with wide vertical stripes in a rainbow of pastel-frosting colors and a pale-yellow floor that reminded Addie of butter. The display and the store had all the delight of a child's candy-store dream, and to top it off, a heavenly sweet aroma filled the sidewalk.

"This is so cute," Addie murmured.

Heather was behind the counter helping a man and a girl of five or six who must have been his daughter.

Addie's eyes kept slipping back to the display window. Her gaze came to rest on the box, and several seconds slipped by. Her focus blurred.

And then something clicked.

One of the symbols in her tasseomancy reading. She was looking right at it.

"A dozen little circles," she said. Her gaze sharpened, and she turned to Trey excitedly. "The little circles are donuts!"

"I'm not sure what that means, but it sounds good?"

She nodded vigorously and looked through the window again. Trey didn't know about the tasseomancy, and she wasn't about to tell him. She had no idea where he stood on things of a supernatural nature—*magic* as Kate called them—and wasn't really comfortable going there with him.

"Yes, I think so. I don't know quite what it means yet, but . . ." She reached in her purse for her phone. "I need to call my aunt, if you don't mind."

"No, please go ahead," he said.

She wandered a few steps down the block and watched Trey duck into Glazed.

"Addie, are you okay?" Kate answered, concern clear in her voice.

"Yes. I mean, as much as I can be, given, you know." Addie shook her head to clear her thoughts. "No, I'm calling you because I realized what one of the symbols in my vision is."

"Oh?"

"The little circles, a dozen of them—they're donuts!"

"Donuts . . ." Kate echoed.

"Donuts. Glazed. *Edna*," Addie said, dropping her voice to an urgent whisper. "She was really ticked off about Yuna. I overheard her when she and Heather came in, remember? You could even say Edna was talking in a threatening way about Yuna."

"Oh—oh!" Kate said.

"It fits," Addie rushed on. "The medical symbol for whoever Edna got the fentanyl from, the donuts, the dollar sign for the money that would be lost if the business got shut down, and the last symbol, which was a man and woman getting split apart. That obviously represents Yuna and Kenneth."

"Hmm, okay. But how would Edna have gotten the fentanyl into Kenneth's prescription bottle? That seems like a lot of work, especially for a woman of ill health who needs a scooter to get around."

"Uhh," Addie murmured, thinking. "The pharmacist! Heather is dating a pharmacist. Maybe Edna got him to, I don't know, put the fentanyl into Kenneth's container."

"But that would have targeted Kenneth, not Yuna," Kate pointed out.

Addie slumped. Her aunt was right. The more Addie thought about it, the less the clues seemed to line up to conclusively point at Edna as the murderer.

"Unless Edna and Kenneth were working together to kill Yuna?" Addie suggested uncertainly.

But she didn't completely believe in the theory she was trying to describe. It was just too complicated. Too forced. In her experience as a scientist, the correct explanations for phenomena were usually the simple, mundane ones, not the convoluted, complex ones.

"That doesn't really work, does it?" Addie said, feeling and sounding defeated.

"I don't think so," Kate replied. "But if you're sure the circles are donuts, then it makes sense that one of the Glazed ladies could be involved."

"Maybe it was Heather, then. She didn't chime in with her mother complaining about Yuna, but that doesn't mean Heather wasn't angry about Yuna threatening the donut shop."

"But again, putting the pills in Kenneth's bottle was more likely to harm him than Yuna."

Addie puffed her cheeks and blew out a breath. "You're right. I'm barking up the wrong tree. I think I'm in the right orchard, but I've got the wrong tree."

Kate gave a light little laugh. "Good analogy."

Addie was ready to end the call, but then Kate spoke up again.

"It's funny you mentioned the pharmacist, though," Kate said. "Because he and Heather came in earlier. And now that we've been talking about Heather and Edna, I'm seeing something the pharmacist said to Heather in a slightly new light."

Addie gripped her phone harder, suddenly feeling a little more hopeful.

"What did he say?"

Chapter Fifteen

"WELLLL," KATE DRAWLED HESITANTLY. "THE only reason I would repeat the transaction to you is because you work here, too. You know our interactions with customers are confidential. Not by law, but by social agreement, if you will."

"Of course."

"Okay, so here's what happened," Kate said, lowering her voice, too. "The pharmacist, whose name is Chad, by the way, came in with Heather. She seemed uncomfortable from the get-go, but he sauntered right to me and asked if I had anything for a woman's libido."

Addie scrunched up her face, already imagining where the conversation was going.

"He said he and Heather wanted something to rev up her desires in the bedroom, so, and I'm quoting here, 'she can keep up with me,'" Kate said. "And Heather looked like she wanted to sink into the floor."

Cringing, Addie said, "Poor Heather. That is just ten kinds of awful. How humiliating for her."

"Yeah," Kate said. "This isn't normally the type of thing I'd talk about, but it's you, and they're your customers, too."

"You're the least gossipy person I know," Addie assured her aunt.

"I made a tincture for Heather, and while they were waiting, they chatted over tea at one of the tables," Kate said.

Addie glanced up as she saw Trey emerge from Glazed with a white paper bag in his hand. She waved at him, and he waved back but didn't approach. Instead, he walked the other direction, leaned against a lamppost, and started scrolling on his phone. He was obviously trying to give her privacy, which she appreciated.

"Chad was asking Heather questions," Kate continued. "And I believe they were talking about Glazed. He was asking about profit and revenue, and Heather seemed worried. She was speaking softly, but I believe she said something about fines."

"Do you think the fines were because of Yuna's inspections?" Addie asked. "Health violation fines?"

"I don't know what else they'd be," Aunt Kate said. "I guess they could be tax-related or something like that, but health violations make more sense. Especially given the heated way Edna was talking about Yuna. Heather seemed anxious, and she shushed him. He didn't like that, of course."

"Why of course?"

"Nothing against Heather," Kate said. "But he's clearly the kind of man who wants to be in control. And she, well, doesn't seem the most confident woman."

"Hmm," Addie said. "You heard about Kenneth, right?"

"I did. Shocking, really shocking," Kate said. "But that does put another twist on things."

"It does, and I'm not sure which way it twists them." Addie glanced at Trey. She'd kept him waiting too long. "I need to go, but let's mull it over and talk again, okay?"

"Sounds good, talk soon."

Addie went to Trey.

"So? Was it what you'd hoped?" he asked.

She shook her head. "I don't think so."

When she didn't elaborate, he didn't press. Instead, he held up the bag.

"Donut appetizer?" he offered.

She grinned. "You know, that sounds really good."

They each pulled out an old-fashioned donut and ate as they walked. Addie asked about his shop and music, and he told her about his dream of getting into the music business as a recording artist or at least a professional songwriter.

"I tried for a while," he said with a shrug. "I lived in L.A. for five years, but I never got my big break."

"I'm sorry," she said.

"It's disappointing, but I promised myself that if I didn't get it in five years, I'd move on. So here I am. And it's okay, really, because I always thought it would be cool to have a guitar shop or a music venue. Now, I get to have both."

"That's a really positive way to see it."

"I like Stargaze," he said, looking around. "I love the mountains." He turned to focus on her. "And if I hadn't moved here, I wouldn't have met you."

He looked down, but not before she saw the faint smile touch his lips.

"Well, I hope we'll get the chance to know each other better," she said, suddenly self-conscious. Why was her heart tapping away like that? "But you can always come visit me in prison."

She said it lightly, joking, but he didn't laugh. Instead, he stopped, so she did, too.

"You're not going to prison," he said, his eyes, sometimes gray-green and sometimes hazel, so intent on her face.

Addie looked down, suddenly aware of how close he stood.

Was he going to try to kiss her? Did she want him to?

Yes, she kind of did, she realized.

They had been circling the same block because there were few people about, and therefore Addie didn't have to weather so many stares. They'd actually ended up right in front of Glazed again. The pink neon OPEN sign switched off, drawing Addie's attention. She glanced into the donut store just as the shop lights were flipped off by Edna, it turned out.

Heather was nowhere in sight. But Edna, on her powered scooter, went into the back of the store. The door to the back rooms closed, but not all the way, leaving a sliver of light spilling out.

The next thing Addie saw made her forget about Trey and his beautiful eyes.

"What the . . ." she mumbled, moving closer to the window.

"What is it?" Trey asked.

"Edna," Addie said. "She's the other owner of this place."

Trey's gaze followed hers, and they both watched for a moment.

"There," Addie said as a figure moved past the partially open door. "That was Edna."

"Okay," he said, obviously not seeing the significance.

"She's walking around back there," Addie said. "I mean, walking just fine. Quickly, even."

"And that surprises you?"

"Yeah," Addie said. "She acts so helpless. From what I've seen of her, I never would have guessed she was capable of this."

She squinted through the window as the faint sound of jazz filtered through.

Her mouth fell open. "She's dancing!" Addie exclaimed.

"Oh, whoa, you're right," Trey said.

Edna was back there moving supplies around. At one point, she shimmied past with a big bag of flour in her arms. A heavy-looking bag.

Then, without warning, Edna's face appeared in the doorway and the door slammed shut.

Addie jumped a little. "Do you think she saw us?"

Trey shook his head. "I'm not sure. Maybe. Would that be bad?"

"I don't know. But I think Edna's been playing up her health problems. The physical ones, at least. To me, that didn't look like a woman who's completely dependent on a scooter or a wheelchair to get around."

"I'm getting the sense that this place and its owners might be connected to the killing," he said with an arched brow.

"Possibly," Addie said faintly, looking back through the window. She turned to focus on him. "I'm sorry I'm being so vague and scattered. You must think I'm a bit of a ding-a-ling."

He quirked a smile at her. "Ding-a-ling?"

"That's what Aunt Kate calls people who are, well, less than bright."

"You're anything but a ding-a-ling," he said with a low laugh. His eyes roamed her face for a moment and then rested on her mouth.

Her heart skipped a beat and then took off like a racehorse.

He reached out to brush the edge of her jaw with his fingertips. And then he bent his head and placed a feather-light kiss on her lips. It was delicious and all-too brief.

"I'd never kiss a ding-a-ling," he whispered.

She smiled and laughed softly.

"Want to get some dinner?" he asked, smiling down at her.

She nodded, and he reached for her hand as they walked toward where his pickup was parked.

Even though she would have savored a longer kiss, she was glad he hadn't pushed things. At the moment, her life was too unsteady and uncertain to have a clear head about men. Not to mention that she was only a couple of months out from a broken engagement. As much as she liked Trey, it simply wasn't the time to rush into a relationship, and he seemed to sense and respect that.

They ended up grabbing sandwiches to go and driving up into the east hills, where they parked in a spot overlooking Stargaze.

"It looks so peaceful down there," Addie said, watching the lights twinkle below. "You'd never guess there was a murderer in one of those houses."

After they'd finished eating, Trey drove back to where her car was parked. He walked her across the street but didn't kiss her again.

"Thank you," she said, sliding behind the wheel and looking up at him. "This was exactly what I needed."

On the way back to Chelsea's, the warm glow from spending time with Trey began to fade. By the time Addie pulled up in front of the cottage, her mind had spun back to Glazed, the tasseomancy vision, and seeing Edna dancing around and hauling heavy flour bags.

Inside, Chelsea was watching TV with a light cotton blanket spread over her legs and Lucky nestled on the sofa next to her.

"How was your not-a-date?" she asked.

"It was really good," Addie said. "But now I feel even more muddled about the murder."

Chelsea muted the TV. "What happened?"

Addie explained about the little circles in her vision, recounted her conversation with Aunt Kate, and described seeing Edna moving easily without her scooter.

"It's all trying to point to something," Addie said. "But I can't see what."

"Well, I don't think Edna and Chad the pharmacist were in cahoots to kill Yuna," Chelsea said.

Addie tilted her head. "Why?"

"Remember when we saw him making out with Heather? They didn't want Edna to see. They're dating in secret." Chelsea whispered the last word, giving Addie a wide-eyed conspiratorial look.

"Not *that* secret, seeing as how they went into Wild Rose together today."

"True. But trust me, Edna doesn't know."

"What makes you so sure?" Addie asked.

"Edna wants to control her daughter," Chelsea said. "She doesn't want Heather to have a life of her own. I've observed them together for years, and it's a pretty clear dynamic."

Addie's brows lowered, and she squinted at her friend. "Do you think Edna is faking the extent of her health problems to try to keep Heather under her thumb?"

"Yes, I do."

"Huh. Okay. Well, then, maybe it's Heather and Chad who offed Yuna."

It just wasn't sliding together, though.

Frustration welled in Addie like an internal pressure, a boiling kettle with the lid on too tight and no outlet. She let out an exasperated growl from deep in her throat, jumped up, and started pacing.

"It just doesn't fit, Chels! What am I missing? Where am I going wrong?"

"I'm not sure." Chelsea sighed, her usually cheery face worried. "But you did discover a couple of things tonight, don't lose sight of those. One, the circles in your tea-leaf reading are donuts, and so Glazed is somehow involved. And two, Edna can apparently get around just fine. That *does* make her more suspicious, you know. Before, I might have doubted she was capable of certain things because of her physical limitations."

"Okay, for a moment, let's ignore all the woo-woo stuff—my vision, Kate's vision, hunches, and auras. Let's get back to basics," Addie said, sitting and taking a calming breath. She focused on letting her logical mind take charge. "Motive, means, and opportunity."

"Good idea. Let's start with Kenneth. Even though he's gone, he still could have killed Yuna. Did he have motive, means, and opportunity to kill her?"

Addie nodded. "Yes."

"Okay. Now, Doctor Palbila," Chelsea said.

"Motive, no. He wanted to be with Yuna, not kill her. But if he'd intended to kill Kenneth and not Yuna, by putting the fentanyl in Kenneth's prescription bottle, then yes there was a motive to kill Kenneth. Palbila certainly has means to get his hands on fentanyl. We don't know if he had the opportunity to plant it, but why not? He might have had a key to the Akido's house from when he was having an affair with Yuna. That's all speculation, but it *could* fit, if the intended victim was Kenneth and not Yuna."

Chelsea nodded. "Edna?"

"Yes on motive, though it's not a strong yes. Means, I'm not so sure." Addie tapped her lower lip thoughtfully. "Maybe she has access to fentanyl because she has a prescription for it. Opportunity to give it to Yuna, though? That's a stretch."

"How about Heather?" Chelsea prompted.

"Motive, yes, same as her mother. Means . . . Hm, I guess she could have gotten fentanyl from her pharmacist boyfriend. But putting it into Kenneth's prescription bottle and trusting that he would give it to Yuna rather than taking it himself? Again, that's a stretch."

"So, just looking at motive, means, and opportunity, Kenneth is still the obvious suspect," Chelsea said.

"Yep."

"But that's ignoring all the woo, as you call it. And if we add those clues in, he's almost definitely *not* the murderer."

They both pondered this in silence for a moment.

"Here's the thing, though," Addie said, her tone somber and her voice soft. "I *have* to narrow it down. I don't have much time before court proceedings begin, so if I choose the wrong person to focus on and go off in the wrong direction, I'm going to be in a world of hurt."

The fear was returning, rearing up like a dark storm rolling over the horizon.

"Well, maybe my appointment with Doctor Palbila tomorrow will reveal something helpful," Chelsea said. She spread her hands. "Really, the theory that he intended to kill Kenneth with the fentanyl but accidentally killed Yuna makes a *lot* of sense."

Addie nodded. "That's true. In all the craziness, I nearly forgot you're going to see him. Do you really think you'll be able to tell by his aura if he intended to kill Kenneth but accidentally killed Yuna instead?"

"I do, actually," Chelsea said. "And if he was the one who killed Kenneth in his house, that will leave a very dark stain. Either way, if Doctor Palbila was involved, I think I'll know."

Feeling slightly less scared, Addie reached out and squeezed Chelsea's hand. "I really, really hope you're right."

Chapter Sixteen

ADDIE SLEPT FITFULLY AND WOKE up feeling unrested. But when she remembered Chelsea's appointment with Doctor Palbila, hope rose in Addie's chest like a little bird taking flight.

She pushed back the covers, stretched, and tried to think positive thoughts.

After quickly making the bed and throwing on sweats, she went to the back door with Lucky on her heels and let him out into the yard. Leaving the door cracked open, she returned to the kitchen to get a pot of coffee going.

Chelsea appeared as the machine was percolating, her blond hair swept up into a messy bun.

"Oo, thank you for starting the coffee," Chelsea said, going to the cupboard and pulling out a mug that read *Princess in Training* in a curly font and had a glittery gold crown on it. She smiled, but her eyes were bleary, and Addie knew not to jump into conversation until Chelsea had some caffeine in her system.

Chelsea clutched the mug in both hands, her eyes on the coffee machine as if it were dripping pure gold into the pot.

Once they both had their steaming mugs of coffee with a splash of vanilla creamer, they sat across from each other in the breakfast nook.

"Are you nervous about Doctor Palbila?" Chelsea asked.

Addie tilted her head from side to side, her gaze cast upward as she considered how to put her thoughts into words. "Not so much nervous as trying to think through what each result will mean. If his aura is dark and murdery, then will that be enough to focus on him as the killer? Or, if his aura isn't that of a killer, then where does that leave me?"

"Let's just see how it goes, first, and then we can try to draw conclusions."

Addie straightened. "I do know one thing. I'm going with you to this appointment. After all, he could be our killer."

"I'm sure I'll be fine, but thank you for that," Chelsea said. "Now that you mention it, I would be more comfortable having someone with me."

They each went to their own rooms to get ready for the appointment, which was in forty-five minutes.

Addie put on her usual uniform of jeans, pairing them with a crisp, fitted white V-neck tee. It was a purposely generic outfit, meant to avoid attention. A bit of makeup and a quick touchup with her flatiron, and she was ready to go. As an afterthought, she put on a baseball cap. It might help her feel a little more anonymous to be able to hide under its bill.

While she waited for Chelsea, she closed and locked the back door and then perused her phone.

There was a text from Bennett that made her pulse bump: *Think I've made a breakthrough. Will come to you at noon to explain.*

A breakthrough?

Oh, please, let it be.

And there was a message from Trey: *Good morning, beautiful. I hope today brings good news.*

That made her smile, and the two text messages together seemed to be a positive omen.

She messaged Bennett: *On the edge of my seat until then!*

Thank you for that, and thank you for last night, she texted to Trey.

"What's that smile for?" Chelsea asked as she breezed in.

The cheery, summery smell of her perfume hit Addie's nose and gave her another little lift.

"Oh, just some encouraging texts," Addie said.

"From?"

"Bennett . . . and Trey."

"Ha! I knew something happened with Trey last night," Chelsea said. "Does Bennett have news?"

"It sounds like he does, and he'll be here at noon to tell us."

"Awesome," Chelsea said with a hopeful grin. "Shall we go?"

They got into the yellow bug, leaving the top up because it was still cool, and Chelsea steered them to the east side of downtown.

Remembering how people had seemed to stare the previous night, Addie was happy to have the cover of the convertible top in place. The memory of Trey's kiss surfaced, too, making her insides glow, but her mood cooled when Chelsea pulled into the lot next to the building that housed Doctor Palbila's practice.

"Ready?" Chelsea asked.

"Ready if you are," Addie said.

They went to the office, located on the second floor, and Chelsea checked in with the receptionist while Addie took a seat at the wall near the door. There was one other person in the waiting area, and he was absorbed in his phone and didn't even give Addie a glance. Still, she felt the need to scrunch down in her chair and make herself as inconspicuous as possible. She pulled her cap's bill low on her brow.

Chelsea checked in and got a clipboard with patient forms to fill out.

"Do you want me to go in with you?" Addie whispered when Chelsea sat down. "And by the way, what are you here for?"

"I'd like you to come in, but it's probably better if he doesn't see you. He probably knows by now that you've been accused of killing Yuna. I'm going to tell him I'm looking for a doctor who has a lot of experience with allergies. It's not a lie. My doctor moved away six months ago, and I haven't found a new one yet."

Addie nodded and then ducked her head down when a nurse came to call Chelsea in.

"Be careful," Addie whispered.

"I won't say anything about the case," Chelsea said, rising. "I'm just here to get a good look at his aura."

Addie tried not to shift around nervously in her seat as she waited. Everything she knew about the murderer, all the discussions and clues, swirled around in her brain like debris in a dust devil.

By the time Chelsea emerged from the exam room, Addie had decided it would be the best possible scenario if Doctor Palbila did turn out to be the murderer. The story was a simple one: Palbila had intended to kill Kenneth, but Yuna had died instead when she'd taken Kenneth's headache medicine that had been replaced with fentanyl. And then, to cover his tracks, Palbila had broken into the Akido home to take the pill bottle. Maybe he hadn't intended to kill Kenneth, or maybe, in Palbila's grief, he wanted to see his real target dead.

It worked.

It worked nicely.

But only if Addie ignored her own tasseomancy vision.

She might have been able to ignore all that woo-woo stuff she was apprehensive about anyway, if not for one fact: her tea-leaf reading had led her to discover who had tried to kill Aunt Kate. And the reading hadn't been wrong then. In fact, it had been a vital part of putting Kate's attacker away.

So, could Addie ignore her own visions?

She stood as Chelsea appeared and quickly checked out.

"Did he do it?" Addie whispered urgently.

Chelsea grabbed her arm. "Let's wait until we're in the car."

They hurried down the stairs and jumped into the VW bug. Addie turned to her friend, holding her breath in anticipation.

"There was a lot of stuff swirling around, and some of it was dark," Chelsea said. "But it's not the aura of a murderer."

Addie slumped and leaned her head back against the headrest.

"I really wish I had a pillow right now," she said.

"How come?"

"So I could scream into it."

"I know, hon, I'm sorry," Chelsea said. "But I'm not completely surprised. I don't think Doctor Palbila has any connection at all to Glazed."

"Maybe I'm wrong about the dozen little circles."

Chelsea shook her head. "You're not. That was a hit of intuition you had, and it was right."

"How do you know?"

"I could tell by the way you talked about it. Things like tasseomancy and auric readings aren't based on thinking and logic." Chelsea placed one hand on her lower abdomen and the other over her heart. "They're about gut feelings and instincts. And those deserve to be honored at least as much as the rational mind. Maybe more."

"But it would be so much easier if I could forget the little donuts," Addie whispered. "Just leave them out completely."

Chelsea gave her a sympathetic look. "Let's get back home. You can check in with Kate, and then Bennett will come."

"Oh, shoot," Addie said. "You're supposed to be at work! It's fine if you need to go."

"I've got Lang there for the morning, but I should probably go so I can relieve her for lunch."

After dropping Addie at the cottage, Chelsea headed out to her boutique.

Once inside, Addie tried calling Aunt Kate. When she didn't pick up, Addie dialed the number for Wild Rose Teas and Apothecary, but Kate didn't answer the store phone either.

After fifteen minutes, Addie tried again. Still no answer.

Worry pinged in her middle, and she wasn't sure if it was from her overall heightened anxiety or if it was a signal that something really was wrong.

Remembering what Chelsea had said about honoring instincts, Addie called Trey. He picked up after the first ring.

"Hey, Addie." His voice sounded strained, which was unusual for Trey.

"Hi, Trey. I was wondering if you could do me a huge favor. If you're at your store, that is. I've been trying to call Kate, but she's not answering. She might just be busy with customers, but could you take a peek in the window and tell me if she's okay?"

"I was just going to call you, actually. There's something going on outside. It looks like some kind of protest."

Addie's heart dropped.

"Oh, no. Please tell me it's not in front of Wild Rose," she said.

"It looks like it is. Hold on, let me go see. Let's switch to video, and I'll show you."

His face appeared on the screen, and she caught a glimpse of the sky as he went outside and shifted his phone in his hand. Trey's face was replaced by the scene on the sidewalk.

There were maybe only ten or twelve people, but they had signs and they looked agitated.

SHUT DOWN THIS POISON STORE! read one sign.

Another read, *Unlicensed and Dangerous*, and there was a marijuana leaf in a red circle with a slash through it.

Marijuana? Kate didn't sell pot. She didn't even carry products with CBD oil, though customers had been asking for them.

Addie squinted, trying to pick out any familiar faces. Her concern flipped to anger when she caught sight of a face she knew all too well: Lisette's.

Trey was making his way past the crowd, moving toward the door to Kate's shop. He opened the door and went in, and the live feed showed Kate inside, alone, and on her phone.

There was a man with her—Marvin, Addie guessed. He was wringing his hands and sending worried looks at the front of the shop.

Kate's face was drawn with concern as she spoke into her phone. She ended the call.

"Kate, I have Addie on a video call," Trey said.

The picture jostled as he seemed to hand the phone to Aunt Kate, whose face then filled the screen.

"I saw Lisette out there," Addie said. "I bet she organized this. Did you call the police?"

"Yes, I just got off the phone with the dispatch operator," Kate said. "They're going to send someone to make sure this doesn't get out of hand, but the lady warned me that the protesters have the right to gather on the sidewalk."

"Close the shop, Aunt Kate," Addie urged. "Lock all the doors and shut off the lights. The best thing you can do is just not engage. Those aren't our customers out there, and they don't need a single bit of your attention."

Kate nodded.

"I'll do it," the man next to her said. He looked into the phone and flipped a little wave. "I'm Marvin, by the way. I'd hoped to meet you soon, but under much different circumstances." He flapped a hand toward the front of the shop and grimaced.

"Hi, Marvin," Addie said. "Thank you for helping out. I promise it's not usually this crazy."

She watched Kate hand him a keyring. He straightened his cardigan and set his chin. He was older, about six feet tall, and had a slight stoop to his shoulders. Addie was glad he was there with Kate.

"I'm so sorry this is happening, Aunt Kate," Addie said.

"Well, it's a poor reflection on certain people in this town, that's for sure." One corner of Kate's mouth pulled down in uncharacteristic sadness.

Seeing her aunt that way dragged at Addie's heart. Kate loved Stargaze. She loved her customers and the people of the town. And, for the most part, Stargaze loved her back. Lisette Dubois Kumar was one of the only people who'd ever given Kate any trouble, which made Addie even more sure that the restaurateur was behind the ugliness going on outside Wild Rose at that moment.

"Let's go into the back," Marvin suggested, his voice coming from off screen.

The picture bounced a little as Trey, Kate, and Marvin moved into the back rooms, out of sight of the small mob.

"You can go home, if you want, Marvin," Kate said. "There's nothing more we can do here today, I'm afraid."

"You should go, too, Kate," Marvin said.

Kate pushed her hair back in an agitated gesture. "I wish I could stay here, to, I don't know, keep watch, I guess. I'm not allowed—" Her gaze cut to just above the phone. She must have been glancing at Trey, who didn't know Kate was a Shuffler. "I mean, the store will be fine, and if I'm not here, maybe the crowd will get bored."

She didn't sound particularly convincing, and Addie knew Kate would have preferred to stand her ground and protect her store.

"I'll keep an eye on things," Trey said. "I'll go out the back and around to get back into my place. I've got a security camera I can set up in the window. If anybody gets rowdy, I'll have it recorded."

"Oh, thank you," Kate said. "That's really a load off my mind. And don't hesitate to call if something happens."

Trey switched the view, so his face once again filled the screen. "I'm going to head next door. I'll call you if there's anything to report, okay?"

"Okay, thanks."

They hung up.

Bennett texted to let Addie know he would be a little late, and for some reason that just made her more anxious about everything.

With her stomach in knots, she tucked herself into a corner of Chelsea's soft sofa, pulled her knees up to her chest, and wrapped her arms tightly around them.

Lucky hopped up and sat next to her, leaning comfortingly against her shin.

"This really is a mess, isn't it?" she whispered, stroking his silky, wavy caramel fur.

She turned on the TV and stared at it without really seeing it for a half hour. Then her phone buzzed with a message from Trey.

I didn't want you to be alarmed if you heard it from someone else.

A picture followed. Addie's hand covered her mouth, muffling her squeak of dismay.

Trey had sent a photo of the big front window of Wild Rose. There was an ugly, jagged hole in the glass.

The crowd ran after that happened, but I caught it on video. The cops are going after the guy who did this. And don't worry about the damage. Kate gave me a key, and I'm going over there now to board up the window.

The phone rang. It was Kate.

"Did Trey tell you?" Addie asked with a lump in her throat.

"Yes," Kate said, her voice heavy and sad. "I'll file an insurance claim, and it'll get fixed. Sounds like Trey caught the guy on video, too, so that's good."

"I just can't believe people are being so awful," Addie said.

"I know. Me too." Kate let out a long sigh. "Addie, I've got to do something I really don't want to do, but I think it's best."

"What?"

"I'm closing Wild Rose."

Chapter Seventeen

"OH NO, PLEASE DON'T DO that," Addie protested.

But even as she said it, she knew Kate had made up her mind. Addie wished she could help. She wished she could do something, anything. But she wasn't even allowed in the shop. Not being able to set foot in Wild Rose Teas and Apothecary made her feel almost sick with helplessness.

"It's best for now," Kate said. "Hopefully it won't be for too long. And maybe I'll put a note on the door so anyone who really needs something can call me for an appointment. I haven't decided about that yet."

"Let me know if I can do anything," Addie said.

The offer had come out automatically, and it was only after she'd said it that she realized how hollow it was. She couldn't do anything for Aunt Kate. Not really.

"Okay. Talk to you soon."

They hung up, and Addie buried her face in her folded arms. She tried to hold back the tears, but they leaked out from her closed eyelids.

When her life in San Francisco had imploded, Stargaze was the only place Addie could dream of going. It was the only place she knew she'd feel safe. Aunt Kate and Wild Rose were a familiar comfort that held a special, precious place in Addie's heart. She knew her aunt would take Addie in and reassure her in exactly the way she needed. And reconnecting with Chelsea had just been the icing on the cake.

Addie was still grappling with her supernatural abilities, but she'd started to settle into a life that felt good. Warm and even safe, despite what'd happened to Aunt Kate and her own struggle to adjust to her new way of life.

But then Yuna Akido had died, and Addie's life had collapsed all over again.

Even worse, she'd dragged Kate and her wonderful shop down, too.

It was like Addie had started to wake up from a bad dream, only to be plunged into an even more terrible nightmare. Somehow, Kate having to close down Wild Rose felt worse than being accused of killing someone.

A knock at the door made Addie jump.

Bennett. She'd almost forgotten.

Swiping her fingers under her eyes, she inhaled sharply, trying to quickly pull herself out of her funk. There wasn't time to glance in the mirror.

She opened the door.

"Hi—" Bennett stopped short when he caught sight of her face, and his expression folded into one of concern, his brows lowering over his dark eyes. "What's wrong?"

Tears threatened again, and Addie fanned her face with one hand, as if that would stop the waterworks.

"It's—it's Wild Rose," she said haltingly. "Kate is closing the store, and I just feel so *bad*."

She swung the door wide, and he stepped in.

"Sorry, I need to grab a tissue," she said, glad for a reason to escape for a moment.

She ducked into the bathroom, where she blew her nose and dabbed at her eyes. A glance in the mirror showed tearstained cheeks, ponytail askew, and red-rimmed eyes.

Oh well, nothing to do about it now.

Bennett had closed the door but was still waiting in the small foyer when Addie returned.

"Come, let's sit down," Addie said, leading him to the sofa where she took her same spot in the corner. "Sorry, I didn't mean to do that. I just talked to her, and she sounded so sad. I can't even think about the money she's losing while the store is closed."

"Not closed for good?" he asked, his concern deepening.

"No, that's not what she's intending. But, well . . ." She launched into the story of the protesters, ending with the hole in the window.

Bennett's hands curled into fists, and he sat perfectly still for a moment.

At times, Addie thought she'd come to know Bennett fairly well. They'd talked so many times, and he was one of only a very few who knew about her tasseomancy. He'd helped her and Kate in ways that no one else could. But in that moment, when he tensed up, there seemed to be a capacity for intensity that bordered on anger lurking under the surface. Addie didn't think it was anything bad or to fear, just a side he kept hidden.

Bennett loosened his fingers and took a breath.

"It sounds like the police know who to charge in the matter of the window," he said. "Kate will be able to press charges if she wants to."

Addie nodded, but that didn't make her feel better. She knew Kate was probably too nice to press charges. Addie waved her fingers through the air, as if physically dispelling the topic of the vandalism of Wild Rose Teas and Apothecary.

"Let's talk about what you've found," Addie said.

"I'll start with this," he said. "I'm almost certain Kenneth isn't the killer."

Addie's brows rose.

Was this good news or bad? Maybe good. Definitely good if Bennett knew who the murderer was.

"I discovered he'd decided not to divorce Yuna," Bennett continued. He quirked a grim smile. "And I know what you're thinking. Maybe he decided not to divorce Yuna because he was going to kill her instead. But it appears to be a real change of heart. Yuna had never wanted children, but he did. She'd changed her mind, though, and they'd talked about it. They were going to recommit to their marriage. They'd even booked a venue for a small ceremony to renew their vows."

Who had given him this intimate information? Addie could ask, but she knew he wouldn't want to disclose his source, and so she decided not to put him in that awkward position.

"Hmm, that's quite a turn," Addie murmured, taking it in. "We know from what Kate told us that Yuna really was trying to get pregnant, so your info seems solid." She chewed the inside of her cheek for a second. "Okay, so is this good? And I'm seriously asking you because I can barely even think anymore."

She gave a thin laugh that was meant to lighten the mood, but it didn't come off the way she'd intended.

He pressed his lips together, his deep-brown eyes softening as he cast her a sympathetic look.

"Any definitive information is good, I think," he said. The tip of his tongue showed between his lips, and his energy seemed to heighten.

Addie straightened, sensing something important was coming.

"You know who it was," she said.

"Not quite. But I think I've narrowed it down to two people. Chad Caravelli or Frank Palbila."

Addie sucked in a breath. "The pharmacist or the doctor." She shook her head. "It's not Palbila."

Bennett's eyes sharpened on her. "What makes you say that?"

"Chelsea and I paid him a visit this morning. Well, she had the appointment. I stayed in the waiting room."

Addie went on to describe the theory about the auras and what Chelsea had discovered in her encounter with the doctor.

Bennett leaned forward, and he propped his elbows on his knees. Looking at her from under his brows, his gaze intensified.

"And what do your instincts tell you?" he asked.

She quieted for a moment, trying to focus on her internal knowing, that place between gut and heart that Chelsea often referred to.

"I think we're on the right track," Addie said slowly. "It wasn't Doctor Palbila. I think it could have been the pharmacist, but something just . . . doesn't quite fit."

He regarded her for a long moment, seeming to soak in her answer. She liked how seriously he took her words, how he truly seemed to value her opinion even though as a P.I. he had vastly more experience with this sort of situation.

"I agree," he said firmly.

Addie's heart bumped, and her spirits lifted the tiniest bit.

"Okay," she said nodding. "Okay, this is good. But it's also bad, because unless you have another surprise for me, we don't have a solid motive for Chad. Why would he have killed Yuna?" She squinted into the distance for a moment. "Or actually, we should probably ask why he would want to kill *Kenneth*, since that's whose pill bottle was filled with fentanyl."

Bennett sat back, crossing one arm over his chest and propping the other fist under his chin in a thoughtful pose. His gaze came to rest on a spot on the carpet. But then after a few seconds, he popped to his feet.

"Do you mind if I walk around?" he asked. "I find it easier to think if I'm moving."

Addie lifted her palm. "Be my guest. I tend to pace when I'm agitated, so I get that. And I just thought of something. Chelsea was with me when we saw Chad and Heather canoodling in the donut shop. I'm going to call Chelsea to see if she remembers anything about Chad's aura. Be right back."

She went to the kitchen with her phone, where she poured two tall glasses of iced tea as she called Chelsea.

"Hey, I hope this isn't a bad time," Addie said.

"No, a couple of customers just left. What's up?"

Addie summarized her conversation with Bennett.

Chelsea gasped dramatically. "Am I hearing you correctly? You, Ms. Scientist Addie James, are willing to put your money on a suspect when there are still some logical gaps?"

"I know, it's so unlike me," Addie said with a faint grin which quickly faded as reality settled in again. "But the thing is, we've got to fill those gaps in fast. Chad obviously has means and opportunity to get those pills into Kenneth's prescription bottle, but we still don't know why he did it. And I think we have to assume that killing Yuna was an accident, Kenneth was the real target, and therefore Chad was the one who went to the Akidos later and killed Kenneth."

"Right, okay."

"I have a specific reason for calling you, though," Addie continued, getting back on track. "Did you see Chad's aura that time when we were watching him and Heather through the window at Glazed?"

She held her breath in anticipation of Chelsea's answer. And even in that second or two, Addie realized how crazy it was that she was pinning so much hope on what someone's *aura* looked like.

Maybe I've really and truly lost it.

"I don't remember seeing anything in particular," Chelsea said. "They were probably too far away, and at the time I was focused on the fact that they seemed to be having a secret fling. I just wasn't thinking about auras. It's kind of like when you pass someone on the street and you notice their face, but you weren't thinking about their shirt, and so you didn't put your focus into what color shirt they were wearing. You might have noticed it, but you might have just as likely not noticed it at all."

"Well, that's easy enough to remedy," Addie said. "We can just pay a little visit to the pharmacy. If Chad put the fentanyl in the bottle and later killed Kenneth, that's two murders. That's got to leave a pretty dark smear on a person's aura, right?"

"For sure. I'll wrap things up early here and get Lang set to close without me, and I'll swing by to pick you up," Chelsea said. "We can go to the pharmacy together."

"Great, just shoot me a text when you leave the boutique, and I'll be ready."

Addie went back into the living room, where Bennett was staring out the front window, and passed him one of the glasses. He absently took a sip of iced tea.

"Chelsea couldn't see Chad's aura," Addie said. "But we're going to swing by the pharmacy this afternoon so she can get a look."

He nodded and sipped again.

"How did you arrive at Chad, anyway?" Addie asked.

Bennett's mouth worked for a second, as if he wasn't quite sure how he wanted to respond.

"Well . . . it was partly logic and partly . . ." He trailed off.

Addie tilted her head. "What?"

He suddenly looked uncomfortable, reaching up with his free hand to rub at the back of his neck in an agitated gesture.

She smiled. "C'mon, it can't be weirder than reading tea leaves or auras," she said lightly.

"It might be," he mumbled.

"Oh," she said. "Well, if you're not comfortable talking about it, that's okay."

But she really, really wanted to know. In fact, she was practically itching with curiosity.

She went to sit down, and he joined her, setting his glass on a coaster.

"You know I've been buying a remedy from Kate for years," he said.

She nodded.

"Do you remember what it was for?"

"I don't think we ever talked about it specifically," she said. "But when I made it for you that one time, from the ingredients I would guess it's for insomnia."

"Right," he said. "I sometimes have trouble getting good sleep because I can—I can leave my body."

"I'm not sure what that means," she said slowly, trying to keep her tone neutral.

"When I'm in a light sleep, I can travel," he said. "Some call it astral projection."

Her brows popped up. "Oh. Oh, I see. I've heard of that."

But I sure as heck never thought it was real. I never believed in reading tea leaves either, though.

"You, uh, astrally projected and learned something about Chad?" she asked.

"Something like that, yes." He puffed his cheeks, blowing out a breath, and slowly rubbed his hands together, still seeming ill at ease. "Is this too weird? I don't have to talk about it."

"Are you kidding? There's not much I would consider 'too weird' at this point," she said, sitting back down on the sofa and gesturing for him to join her. "So can you ghost around and see what people are doing, or what?"

He perched on the edge of the cushion. "Not exactly. It's more like eavesdropping on their dreams. And when I'm able to get into a person's dream, I can sometimes also see their memories."

"Huh," she said, trying her best not to shift uncomfortably.

"Don't worry, I would never do it to you," he said hurriedly. "I don't spy on people. I never do it, really. Well, almost never. It's just that the ability to do it can really disrupt my sleep."

"It's all right, Bennett, really," she said. "I didn't think you were snooping in my memories. You're not that kind of person. It's probably why you have this ability, because you're not the type to abuse it."

That brought a small smile, and he seemed to relax slightly.

"I only did it this time because I thought it might help us," he said. He took a breath. "I visited both Doctor Palbila's and Chad Caravelli's dreams last night. I think I might have learned something useful from Chad."

She leaned forward a little in anticipation. "Were you able to see his memories?"

Bennett nodded. "I believe he intended to murder someone, but I don't think it was Yuna or Kenneth."

Chapter Eighteen

"WAIT, WHAT?" ADDIE ASKED, NOT believing she'd heard correctly. "You don't even think Kenneth was the intended victim?"

"No," Bennett said. "I think that was a mix-up."

"Then who was Chad trying to kill?"

"I don't know," Bennett said. "In Chad's memory, he was in the pharmacy filling prescription bottles. There were a couple of empty ones on the counter. They had labels, but the labels were turned away. He got distracted for a second. I think he put the fentanyl into the wrong container."

"Wow," Addie said. "But maybe the whole thing was accidental. Just a terrible mistake."

"Nuh uh," Bennett said. "He definitely meant to kill someone."

"How do you know?"

"Because I accessed another memory. In that one, he was having a phone conversation. I don't know who he was talking to because the person he called wasn't identified by name, but Chad said, 'Things are about to get a lot better because that witch is going to be dead and out of our hair very soon.'" Bennett grimaced. "Only, he didn't say 'witch.'"

"Wow," Addie said again. She swallowed hard. "So, by what you said, his intended victim was a woman. But you're sure it wasn't Yuna?"

"I'm sure, and that's just logic speaking," Bennett said. "As we already figured out, Yuna as the victim just doesn't make sense when it was Kenneth's pill bottle."

"Right," Addie agreed. "So, do we even need to figure out who Chad really meant to kill? Isn't it enough to just prove he was the source of the pills that caused Yuna's death?"

"Maybe, in an ideal world. But sneaking into people's memories isn't exactly the kind of evidence I can present to the police."

Addie slumped. "Right. Same with tea leaves and auras."

"You and Chelsea should still check out Chad and see if his aura confirms what I learned, though," Bennett said. "And I'll work on figuring out how we can get Chad on the radar as a strong suspect."

Addie saw Bennett to the door and watched him drive away. She felt momentarily lifted by their conversation, but then she realized they didn't have any hard information and her hopes came sailing right back down. They didn't have anything that would take the focus off her as the killer.

They had to either get Chad to confess or get someone else to provide proof that he had murderous intentions and that Kenneth ended up with the wrong prescription that resulted in a tragic end for his wife, and later, for Kenneth too.

And that reminded Addie of the intruder who killed Kenneth Akido in his home. It had to be Chad. Maybe that was the place to start. If Chad was identified as Kenneth's killer, then Chad could fall under suspicion for Yuna's death.

Maureen, Addie's lawyer, called not long after Bennett left. The purpose of the call was to touch base with Addie and let her know when she'd be expected in court again. Unfortunately, that would be late the next afternoon, when Addie would be formally charged and would have to enter her plea.

"Which will be . . ." Maureen prompted.

"Not guilty, of course," Addie said, her tone going tense and cross. "There is absolutely no way my herbal remedy caused Yuna any harm. I did *not* kill anyone!"

Addie had hoped that by some miracle the police would have realized she couldn't possibly be the killer. Or even better, they'd come up with a stronger suspect. Given the late hour, it was extremely unlikely either of those things would happen before Addie was due to appear before the judge.

"Of course, of course," Maureen said soothingly. Her tone was placating but gave no indication she actually believed Addie, which only made her more irritated. "And you're steering clear of any amateur detective activities, right?"

Addie made a face and crossed her fingers behind her back. "Of course, of course," she said, echoing her lawyer.

She knew she was being childish, but it really aggravated her that Maureen seemed to think there was a possibility Addie was guilty.

"Maureen, I have a very clear alibi for the time Kenneth Akido was killed. Doesn't that cast doubt on me being Yuna's killer?"

"It may. But this isn't the time for presenting a bunch of evidence. That will come later. Meet me outside the courthouse fifteen minutes early tomorrow," Maureen said.

"Okay, thanks. Will do."

Addie hung up and then stalked around the house for a few minutes, trying to cool her temper.

Chelsea arrived home, and Addie's mood immediately lifted at the sight of her friend.

"How was work?" Addie asked.

"Honestly, I was antsy all afternoon, and I'm glad I was able to leave early," Chelsea said. She flopped on the sofa for a second, but then she sprang up and went to get her purse, which she'd hung on the hook by the door. "You know what? I think we should go to the pharmacy right now. I'm not going to be able to calm down until I get a look at Chad Caravelli's aura."

"Oh, good," Addie said. "Bennett and I realized that is priority one. And wait until I tell you why he believes Chad is definitely the killer."

"Let's get on the road, and then you can tell me."

Once they were settled in Chelsea's yellow VW bug, Addie started to tell her about the conversation with Bennett. But then Addie hesitated.

"I'm not sure if I should be revealing this," Addie said, glancing at her friend.

"You mean the astral projection and dreamwalking?"

Addie's mouth fell open. "How'd you know?"

"He and I have talked about it a little," Chelsea said.

"When? Why?" Addie asked, frowning. For some reason, she didn't like that Chelsea knew about this first. Bennett and Chelsea hadn't even known each other until they'd met through Addie.

"Don't be hurt," Chelsea said. "He only talked about it because I sensed he had a supernatural ability. I told him about how I can read auras, and that made him comfortable enough to talk about his abilities."

Addie wanted to know why Bennett hadn't wanted to talk to her about those things, but she already knew the answer.

"People sense your skepticism," Chelsea said gently. "But it's not a bad thing. Being logical is not a flaw."

"Around here it kind of feels like it is," Addie said in a small voice.

"Look, he really likes you, Addie. I can *see* it, both in the mundane sense and the auric sense. He took a big risk talking about his magic with you. He wanted you to know."

"You mean he's . . . interested in me?" Addie asked. "Aunt Kate seemed to think so, but she's an eternal optimist and kind of a romantic, and I'm not, of course, especially not after Jeremy, and . . . you really think so?"

"For sure," Chelsea said with a light laugh. "But please don't ever tell him I can see it so clearly. I don't think he'd appreciate that." She cast Addie a look. "Is the feeling mutual?"

Addie bit her lip for a second. "Yeah, it is. I mean, with the caveat that I don't think I'm ready for anything serious yet. But yes, I am interested in him. I just . . . well, I barely heard from him after Aunt Kate's attacker was caught and figured if there'd been anything there it was either in my imagination or it was a passing thing on Bennett's part."

"Are you more interested in Bennett than Trey?"

Trey. The kiss. She'd definitely enjoyed her date with Trey. He was soulful, he had that musician's voice that sent a little tingle down her spine, he was caring in an easy kind of way, and he was so good-looking.

But he wasn't Bennett, and for reasons Addie couldn't pinpoint, her mind always snagged on Bennett.

She thought about Chelsea's question.

If I had to choose, which one . . . ?

Addie felt her cheeks heating slightly. She shook her head. "I think—" She shook her head. "I don't know what to think now."

Chelsea patted Addie's knee. "That's totally fine. You have other, bigger things to focus on right now anyway."

Understatement of the year.

"Let's talk about you," Addie said.

"What do you mean?"

"Men. You know, love. All that stuff."

"Oh, I don't have anything serious going right now," Chelsea said, shaking her head a little, which sent her waves of blond hair tumbling around her shoulders.

"But what do you want?" Addie asked.

Chelsea scrunched her mouth to one side for a moment. "You know, lately I've kinda been thinking about *marriage*." She said the word as if she'd just declared she wanted to become an astronaut.

"I can totally see you with a husband and kids," Addie said.

"Really?"

"Yeah. You're so warm and caring. Why does it feel strange to be thinking that way?"

"Probably because of my parents," Chelsea said quietly. "I don't remember much about my mom, but I know my parents didn't get along well. And—and I think because I was an only child, and because my dad was . . . the way he was, I've always felt like maybe they didn't really want kids. Maybe I was an accident." She shrugged. "All of it didn't exactly paint family life in the best light."

"But that's why it would be so wonderful if you had your own family," Addie said. "You could do it all differently."

"True."

"You haven't mentioned anybody in your life. Are you seeing someone in secret?" Addie asked it in a lighthearted tone, but she realized that Chelsea had been rather quiet about her personal life lately.

"Oh no, no secret affairs. There really isn't anyone, which I guess makes it a little silly that I've got marriage on the brain."

"Not at all," Addie said. "Who knows, maybe you just put something out there and now the universe is going to start conspiring to send someone your way."

Chelsea laughed. "That sounds like something I'd say."

"You must be rubbing off on me," Addie said with a grin.

Her mood turned serious when she realized where they were.

Chelsea steered into the parking lot of the grocery store where Chad Caravelli's pharmacy was located, and Addie's stomach tightened.

"Okay, how are we going to do this?" Addie asked.

Chelsea pulled into a parking spot near the little corral for empty carts and shut off the bug's engine.

"You're going to have to stay out of sight since you've been accused of the murder he may have committed."

Addie frowned. "I don't like the idea of you going in there to talk to him alone."

"I won't be alone." Chelsea gestured at the other cars in the lot. "There are tons of people in there."

Still not liking the idea of Chelsea facing Chad by herself, Addie pressed, "What are you going to do when you get to the pharmacy?"

"I'll, um, oh! I know. I'll ask for some of that allergy medicine they keep behind the counter. And then if Chad's not within sight, I'll say I've never used it before and I need a consult with the pharmacist."

"I guess that will work," Addie said reluctantly.

"I'll be fine," Chelsea said. "It's not like I'll be alone with him or anything."

"Um, yeah, if he asks you to go into one of those little rooms where they sometimes do flu shots and whatnot, you better run."

"I'm not going to run; that would blow my cover," Chelsea said with wide-eyed exasperation.

"Then walk fast. Scream if he grabs you. Promise?"

"He's not going to grab me." Chelsea shook her head and looked skyward.

"Just promise me."

"I promise I will run and or scream if things get dicey."

"Thank you."

"You going to stay in the car?" Chelsea asked, reaching for her purse in the back seat.

"I guess," Addie said with another frown, for some reason not liking how far the bug was parked from the grocery store's entrance. "If you're not out in ten minutes, I'm coming in."

"Make it fifteen. There could be a line or something." Chelsea squeezed Addie's forearm. "Relax, it's going to be okay. All I'm trying to do is get a look at him. I'm not going to march in there and accuse him of murder or anything."

Addie let out a breath. "You're right. Okay. Good luck."

She watched her friend walk across the lot and disappear into the store, and then Addie checked the time so she'd know when exactly fifteen minutes had elapsed.

"Better yet, I'll set a timer," she mumbled.

Logically, she knew there was almost no chance any harm would come to Chelsea inside the store. But Addie hated the idea of her friend talking to a potential murderer by herself, even with a pharmacy counter between them.

Addie anxiously watched people go in and out of the store for the next six minutes and seventeen seconds.

A text from Chelsea popped up.

Everything's good. I'm in line. Hoping I can get a look when I get up there.

Are you sure he's there? Addie texted back.

It would be just her luck if Chad wasn't working that night.

His name is on the plaque as the pharmacist on duty now.

Addie chewed on her thumbnail as she waited for an update.

About five minutes later, she saw Chelsea emerge from the store. She hurried across the lot to the bug, jumped inside, tossed her purse and a plastic shopping bag in the back, and turned to Addie.

"So?" Addie said, spreading her hands. "What did you see?"

"An aura filled with darkness," Chelsea said, her voice low and her eyes wide. "It was . . . haunting." She hugged herself.

Addie let a slow breath out through her parted lips. "He did it, then?"

"Either that or he's done some other very, very horrible thing recently."

Chelsea closed her eyes and shivered a little.

"I'm sorry you had to see that, Chels."

"It's okay. I'll be fine in a while." Chelsea opened her eyes. "Now we know. That's what matters."

"We do, thanks to you." Addie pushed her hair back, securing it behind her ears. "You think he killed both Yuna and Kenneth?"

"Yes," Chelsea said grimly. She gripped the steering wheel and looked out through the windshield. "There were two very black areas of his aura. And frankly, there were other dark areas, too."

"You think he's killed other people?"

"Maybe not, but this is not a good person we're dealing with."

"Wow. That's really disturbing." Addie's concern deepened when she recalled seeing Heather and Chad making out in the donut shop. "I'm concerned about Heather."

"That's really sweet of you, and you're probably right to be worried about her," Chelsea said. "But we need to come up with some hard evidence."

Addie's insides tightened. "I know. All these things—auras, tea leaves, astral projection—they're no help when it comes to the police."

Chelsea shook her head forlornly. "All of it screams the name of the killer, and yet that voice is silenced because our proof isn't *real* proof."

"If we had a witness or someone Chad confessed to, then we'd have something concrete," Addie said.

They looked at each other.

"Are you thinking what I'm thinking?" Chelsea asked.

"I'm not psychic that I know of, but yes."

"Heather," they both said at the same time.

Chapter Nineteen

"WHERE SHOULD WE GO TO find Heather?" Addie asked. "Should we try Glazed?"

"Yeah, let's try there," Chelsea said, starting the VW bug and steering out of the grocery store parking lot. "The most important thing is to talk to her when Chad's not there."

"Right. I wish I knew what time he gets off work." She pulled her phone from her purse. "I'm going to call Bennett to tell him about the aura really quick."

Bennett picked up after the first ring, and Addie gave him a brief rundown. She also explained where she and Chelsea were headed.

"I don't suppose you know Chad's work schedule, do you?"

"Wish I did, but I don't," Bennett said. "And for that reason, I don't think it's a good idea to confront Heather."

"I thought you might say that," Addie said. Her stomach was churning with nerves, but she tried to keep her voice calm. "But the thing is, we don't have the luxury of time. I mean, *I* don't have the luxury of time. I need something concrete to give to the police, and I need it now."

"I don't disagree," Bennett said. "But I still think it's dangerous."

"What if we ask Heather to come with us somewhere else?" Addie suggested. "Like Chelsea's house or some neutral ground with people around?"

"That would make me feel a lot better about this." He sounded genuinely relieved. "I would offer to meet you there, but I'm in the middle of something and can't leave right away."

"Oo, is it a stakeout?" Addie asked, half-joking.

"Actually, yes."

"Oh," she said, surprised. But of course Bennett would have other jobs. He was a professional P.I., not just a volunteer detective working on her case. "If you want to come by when you're done, we can fill you in on Heather."

She looked to Chelsea for confirmation, and she gave a quick nod.

"It might be late."

"That's okay," Addie said. "I don't think I'm going to be sleeping much tonight, anyway."

"Good luck, and please be on the lookout for Chad."

"Will do." Addie ended the call and turned to Chelsea. "He doesn't want us to confront her."

"That's understandable. He's just looking out for us. For you." Chelsea smiled briefly.

"Let's try to get her to come with us to someplace Chad wouldn't go. I'm trying to think of a spot she wouldn't object to." Addie tapped her bottom lip.

"Pretty sure he wouldn't show up at the police station," Chelsea said drily.

Addie let out a short, humorless laugh. "True. But unless Heather has an urgent desire to confess something about Chad's crimes, that'll just freak her out."

"I know, I wasn't seriously suggesting it, but a girl can hope."

Chelsea pulled up in front of Glazed, and to Addie's huge relief, the lights were still on inside even though the pink neon OPEN sign had been turned off. She saw someone moving around in the back.

With her pulse tapping a nervous rhythm, Addie got out of the bug and went to the door and knocked, cupping her hands to peer inside. Chelsea came to stand beside her.

A silhouette of a woman in an electric scooter appeared in the doorway leading from the back room to the storefront.

"It's Edna," Addie murmured.

She waved.

Edna stopped halfway to the door. "We're closed!"

"I know! Please wait! I need to speak to Heather, and it's urgent," Addie hollered desperately as Edna began maneuvering her scooter to turn around. "It's an emergency!"

The scooter paused, angled toward the door, and moved forward.

"What's the emergency?" Edna asked through the glass.

Addie's mind spun. She didn't want to out Heather's relationship with Chad, and Addie also wanted to keep the whole murder-suspect thing under wraps for the moment. "It's, uh, private. Is Heather here?"

"No," Edna said. She flattened her lips into a line. "Girl dumped hot icing all over her pants, shirt, and shoes, so she ran home for a change of clothes."

"Is she coming back?"

"She well better," Edna said. "We've got to finish inventory tonight."

Addie glanced at Chelsea. They really needed to speak to Heather alone, and Addie didn't want to try to do it in or near the donut shop because Chad might show up.

"Could you call her and ask her to meet me at a location on the way?" Addie asked. "It's really important."

Edna frowned. "No. I need her here, and I don't want her fiddle-diddling around with the likes of you. If you want to talk to her so bad, you can wait for her to show up."

Addie growled deep in her throat. This woman wasn't just being uncooperative; she was downright rude.

"Edna," Chelsea said, a sweet smile on her face. "I'm very concerned about Heather's safety, and I need to speak to her right away. Could I please have her phone number?"

Edna crossed her arms and gave Chelsea a grumpy glare. "Why don't you just tell me what this is about?"

"I'm sorry. I'd rather not say," Chelsea said. "I don't want to violate her privacy."

"She's my daughter. There's no need for privacy."

Well, that says a lot about Heather and Edna's relationship, Addie thought irritably.

"We think she's mixed up with someone dangerous," Addie said. "Very dangerous."

"Who?" Edna demanded.

"It's a . . . personal relationship," Chelsea said.

Edna let out a bark of a laugh. "What, a boyfriend or some nonsense? That girl doesn't have a boyfriend, believe you me."

"She is involved with a man," Addie said, trying to stay calm. "And he's not a good person."

"And why should I trust the word of an accused killer?" Edna demanded. "In fact, if you don't get away from my store, I might just have to call the police."

She reached toward the basket in front of the scooter's handlebars, where there was a cell phone and a pocket pack of tissues.

Addie's stomach plummeted. The last thing she needed was for the police to show up while she was in the middle of a very unauthorized investigation to clear her own name.

"This has gone sideways," Addie whispered to Chelsea, backing away.

"Agreed," Chelsea whispered back.

They turned and retreated to the car, where Chelsea quickly started the engine and drove around the corner, out of view of the donut shop. She pulled to the curb and left the car idling.

"I think we should go around to the other side and watch for Heather," Addie said. "Maybe we can intercept her before she goes inside."

"Good thinking."

Chelsea made a couple of turns and then parked down the street from Glazed, where they could see down the sidewalk that passed in front of the donut shop but weren't visible from the shop's windows.

"Edna is a real treat, isn't she?" Addie muttered, still annoyed about the interaction.

"She's not the most pleasant person in Stargaze by a long shot," Chelsea said. "And she obviously makes things difficult for Heather."

"That poor woman." Addie shook her head. "No wonder she's sneaking around with Chad."

Chelsea took a breath to reply, but Addie cut her off, "Look! There's Heather."

A Honda Civic had just parked on the street perpendicular to where Chelsea's Volkswagen sat, and a woman with long, fluffy hair got out and slammed the door. She hurried across the road toward the building where Glazed was located.

Addie was out of the car in a flash, her pulse jumping as she sprang into a jog.

"Heather," she called, waving. "It's Addie from Wild Rose. Can I talk to you for a sec?"

Slowing, Heather leaned forward, seeming to peer into the darkness. She stopped walking and waited for Addie to cross the street. Chelsea was right behind her.

"Hi," Addie said. She tried to relax, not wanting to spook Heather. "This probably seems kind of weird that I was chasing you down like this."

"It's okay," Heather said, flicking a glance at Chelsea. "Is there a problem?"

"Well, yes, kind of," Addie said but then hesitated. She wasn't sure how to broach the topic of a murderous boyfriend gracefully.

"It's about Chad," Chelsea said. Her voice was soft and disarming in a way that highlighted her sweetness and warmth. Addie knew from past experience Chelsea was good at connecting with people this way.

Heather frowned, the light of the streetlamp highlighting her brow and shadowing her eyes. "What about him?"

"We think he may have done something bad, and we're very afraid you might be in danger," Chelsea said.

Stiffening and drawing in a short breath, Heather looked back and forth between the two women. Addie could almost swear she felt Heather's unease like a physical vibration. But instead of responding, Heather thinned her lips, seeming to bite down on them as if she were afraid of saying anything.

"Do you know what we're talking about, Heather?" Addie asked, trying to match Chelsea's gentle tone.

"I—I don't know," Heather said hesitantly.

"Have you ever heard him say that he might want to hurt someone?" Chelsea pressed softly. "Or maybe just had the sense that he might be dangerous?"

Heather's lips parted, and she was taking shallow breaths through her mouth.

"Are you talking about the—the . . ." She trailed off to a whisper and looked sharply at Addie.

Addie nodded. "Yuna and Kenneth Akido."

Heather frowned and shook her head slightly.

"We often know these things in our hearts or our guts, even as our minds refuse to accept them," Chelsea said. "But in this case, there is no denying that Chad is fully capable of doing terrible things. He's already done them. We're scared for you, and we also need your help."

The poor woman looked very distraught, but she wasn't trying to deny what Addie and Chelsea were suggesting.

"If you know something that would prove Chad's connection to—" Addie started.

"Shh," Heather cut in. She twisted around, looking toward the nearby corner of the building they stood next to. "Did you hear that?"

The three women exchanged wide-eyed looks.

"I didn't hear anything," Addie whispered. Then louder said, "Is someone there?"

She walked a few steps toward the end of the block and nearly shrieked when someone rounded the corner.

When Addie saw who it was, her blood iced over.

It was Chad Caravelli.

He put on an amicable smile, but his eyes narrowed to suspicious slits.

"Hi there," he said casually. His gaze locked on Chelsea. "Didn't I just see you at the pharmacy? That's quite a coincidence."

"It's a small town," Chelsea said with a little laugh that sounded anything but light to Addie's ears.

"That it is," Chad said, strolling slowly toward the women. He lifted his chin at Heather. "Hey, babe. What are you doing standing out here in the dark?"

"Nothing. I was just about to go inside," Heather said, her voice weak and tight.

Chad walked to her and slung a heavy arm across her shoulders, smashing Heather's fluffy hair.

Addie's heart was beating so hard she felt sick. He'd heard them. She knew it. He'd been standing around the corner eavesdropping. If Heather hadn't been in danger before, she surely was then.

And Heather wasn't the only one. If he'd heard the conversation, he knew Addie and Chelsea had found him out as the killer.

With wide eyes, Addie focused in on Heather and tried to send a silent signal that they needed to come up with some reason for Heather to get away.

But Heather was looking down at the ground.

"I'll come with you," Chad said, steering her around. He made eye contact with Addie as he passed. "Small town or not, it's best not to loiter in the dark. The world can be a very, very dangerous place. Deadly, even."

Addie's heart nearly froze. Her gaze whipped to Chelsea. Their eyes locked, and together they turned and ran to the bug. Chelsea fumbled her keys for a moment as she tried to start the engine. But then she just sat with her hands on the wheel.

"We can't just leave her with him," Chelsea said.

"I don't know how to help her, though," Addie said. "Honestly, I almost got the feeling that she doesn't want help, or maybe just doesn't feel like she can accept it. Did you see the way she shrank when he put his arm around her?"

"Yeah," Chelsea said. "He's a controlling jerk; that's pretty clear."

"A controlling jerk and a *murderer*."

"He heard us, didn't he?"

Addie could only nod.

"We can't just sit here," she said after a moment.

"I know, I want to get as far from him as possible," Chelsea said. "But he knows that we know. He's going to come after us. I can't think of a safe place to go. We can't even call the police because we don't even have anything to say to them at this point."

"I'm not allowed to leave town, so I can't go far anyway," Addie said. "I'm going to call Bennett. But first, I want to leave a note on Heather's car. We can at least tell her to reach out if she decides she wants help. She needs to know she has options."

"Good idea." Chelsea reached for her notebook, tore out a page, and printed a short note. "Okay if I put your phone number along with mine?"

"Sure," Addie said.

Chelsea finished the note, folded it, and handed it to Addie.

"I'm going to pull up right alongside her car," Chelsea said.

She rounded the corner, and Addie jumped out, secured the note under one of the windshield wipers, and got back in the car.

Then she pulled out her phone and dialed Bennett, praying he would pick up. He did.

"We have a serious problem," Addie said, her stomach churning with dread and fear.

Chapter Twenty

AFTER ADDIE FULLY RECOUNTED THE conversation with
Heather and then what happened with Chad, there was a long
moment of silence on the phone.

"Bennett? Are you still there?" Addie asked.

"I'm here. I was just trying to think of something reassuring to say."

"Frankly, I'd rather have straight talk than reassurance right now.
How worried should we be?"

"I think we have to assume Chad's going to come after you,"
Bennett said, his voice every bit as grim as Addie felt.

A knot knitted itself tightly in the pit of her stomach.

She was twisting the strap of her purse tightly around her fingers,
so tight it was almost painful. She gripped it hard in her fist, feeling
the fast tap of her pulse in her strangled fingertips.

She'd thought the worst possible thing had already happened. But
it turned out there was something worse than being accused of a
murder she didn't commit; having the true killer find out she knew
what he'd done was far more terrifying.

"Should we call the police?" she asked.

"You could. Maybe you should," Bennett said. "But the problem, and I know you already know this, is that Chad hasn't made any sort of direct threat. He hasn't committed any crime or violence that we can prove. Unless . . ."

"Unless what?"

"Unless you think Heather might have something concrete to say about his part in the murders."

Addie blew out a breath, trying to calm her thumping heart. "I don't know if she does or not. She might have been about to say something. She definitely seemed like something was weighing on her. But for all I know, it may just be a bad gut feeling she's had about Chad. It's entirely possible she doesn't have anything more concrete than we do."

"Where are you headed now?" Bennett asked.

Addie pulled the phone away from her mouth to ask Chelsea, "Where are we going?"

"I don't know," Chelsea said, shaking her head and sending her blond waves tumbling around her shoulders. "I don't know where to go."

"We're just driving around," Addie said into the phone. "We're not sure where to go. I would say Wild Rose because the lower floor is fully alarmed now, but I'm not allowed there. If we're not going to stay at Chelsea's, we have to at least run by there so I can pick up Lucky."

Her chest clenched at the thought of her sweet little dog alone in the house and the possibility of Chad showing up there. She squeezed her eyes closed, hard.

"The two of you should stay with me," Bennett said.

Addie's eyes popped open, and her brows rose. "Uh . . . really?"

"I've got surveillance cameras on every inch of the property. And I've got firearms."

Surveillance and firearms?

How did I get into this mess? Addie couldn't help thinking with a small shake of her head.

"You're probably right," Addie said. "Thank you for offering. We'll run by Chelsea's to grab a few things and get Lucky, and then we'll be on our way to your place."

"I'll meet you at Chelsea's," Bennett said. "If you get there before me, stay in your car."

"Okay, will do. Thank you again."

Addie ended the call and turned to Chelsea.

"I'm so sorry about all of this," Addie said miserably. "First you put up my bail and take me in after I get banned from Wild Rose, and now we have to run for our lives."

"Hey, I offered," Chelsea said. "And I know you'd do the same for me if I got in trouble."

"I would," Addie said without hesitation. "I absolutely would. But I still feel terrible."

"We're going to get through it," Chelsea said. "Chad is going to pay for what he did, and you will be cleared."

"Is that based on some kind of clairvoyant vision you're having?" Addie asked hopefully. She was on the edge of tears, fighting to maintain her composure.

Chelsea cast Addie a faint smile. "It sounds like you want the answer to be yes. Is this really my scientist friend Addie hoping for a magical vision?"

"I know, I know, what's happening to me?" Addie gave a laugh that dissolved into a soft sob. A tear dripped from one eye, and she swiped it away with an impatient brush of her fingers.

"It's not a vision," Chelsea said. "It's confidence that an innocent person is not going to prison for murder. I refuse to accept any other outcome."

"Thank you," Addie whispered, wishing she could feel so confident.

When they turned onto Chelsea's street, Addie's pulse ratcheted up again. She scanned the few cars that were parked in the vicinity.

"Did you see Chad's car when we were outside of Glazed?" she asked. "I don't think I did."

"No, unfortunately," Chelsea said. "He wouldn't be so stupid as to park in plain sight if he came here anyway, though."

"Bennett said to wait for him before we go in," Addie said.

Chelsea pulled up in front of the cottage and killed the engine.

With a cold sweat breaking out over her back and chest, Addie squinted at the dark yard on the right side of the house. Were those just bushes, or was someone lurking there by the house?

"Hey," Chelsea whispered. "What is that on the front door?"

Addie's gaze shifted to the porch, where the outdoor light had been left on, and the door.

"A flyer, I think?" Addie said.

Chelsea leaned forward. "There's something . . . oh!" She stiffened back against the seat. "I think that's a *knife* holding a piece of paper on the door."

"A what?" Addie said, her voice pitched high in alarm.

A car pulled up behind them, making her inhale sharply. But when the car's headlights shut off, she recognized Bennett behind the wheel of his Jeep.

He got out and came up to Addie's window. She reluctantly opened the door and stepped out.

"There's a piece of paper stuck to the front door with a knife," she said, pointing.

Bennett's jaw muscles worked as he whipped around to look. "Please give me the house key," he said, extending his hand back without turning toward Addie. With the other hand, he reached for the holster on his hip and withdrew a gun.

Chelsea passed her keyring to Addie with one key extended, and Addie handed it to Bennett.

"I'm going in to clear the house," he said, his voice pitched deeper and taking on a business-like tone. "Please get back into the car and then wait until I've come out and all the way back here, right next to you. That's how you'll know it's safe. Not if I call. Not if I stand on the porch and wave. Only if I come right back here. Lock the car. This shouldn't take long."

Chelsea hit the power locks as soon as Addie was back in the passenger seat.

She watched Bennett use the key to let himself into the cottage. Lights started coming on throughout the house. That was good, right?

Shaking slightly with nerves and a chill that had come over her, she stared at the house and sent out a silent plea to the universe that Chad wasn't in there, lying in wait.

When she thought of Lucky, she squeezed her eyes closed against the tears that wanted to fill them.

"It's gonna be okay," Chelsea said. "Bennett knows what he's doing. And I don't think Chad's in there, anyway. Any second, Bennett's going to come out, and we'll see Lucky is fine."

All Addie could do was nod and clamp down on her trembling lips.

After about ten minutes that felt like an agonizing eternity, the porch light went on and Bennett emerged from the house with a wiggling, furry bundle in his arms.

Addie scraped at the lock with her fingers, found purchase, and then threw the door open as tears spilled over.

"I know, I know," she said, meeting Bennett halfway on the paved walkway leading to the porch. "I'm supposed to wait in car."

Lucky gave a joyful little bark, and Addie took him in her arms and buried her face in the fur at the back of his neck.

"Thank you," she whispered, looking up at Bennett. She cleared her throat and sniffed hard, trying to compose herself. "Was there anything amiss?"

He shook his head. "No signs that anyone tried to get in. But I think it'd be best if you and Chelsea quickly grabbed a few essentials. The faster we get you somewhere more secure, the better."

"What is that on the door?" Chelsea asked, leaning across the passenger seat to peer at Addie and Bennett.

"A handwritten note," Bennett said, looking back at Chelsea, his gaze then shifting to Addie. "It has your phone number on it, along with another one."

For a second, Addie frowned in confusion. Then she felt the blood drain from her face. "It's the note we left on Heather's car. The one with our phone numbers, telling her to reach out if she wanted to talk or needed help."

She locked eyes with Chelsea, who also looked scared.

"That's a knife driven into it?" Chelsea asked, her voice trembling.

"It is," Bennett confirmed. He took out his phone. "I'm going to take pictures of it. And I think you should report it. It's threatening. Enough to call it in to the police. Now, let's get your things so we can get out of here ASAP."

Addie went back to the bug and put Lucky into the back seat. Chelsea got out, retrieved her keys from Bennett, locked the car, and then she and Addie went with him back into the house.

When they passed the note, which looked like it had a few holes in it as if Chad had stabbed the knife into it multiple times, Addie felt a little dizzy. Anger and violence seemed to emanate from it. Maybe she was picking up a bit of Chelsea's ability to read energy, or maybe it was just that menacing—threatening, as Bennett had said. The knife looked like a folding blade, maybe three inches, and it had a slightly worn leather-wrapped handle. It definitely looked like a man's knife.

"Do you think there are fingerprints?" Addie called to Bennett.

"We can hope. We'll leave it to the police to check. I've got a fingerprint kit, but I don't want to mess with it. It's more important to get the police involved so it's all on official record."

After stepping into the house, Addie thought better of it and stopped, went back to the door, and took a close-up photo of the ugly little message left there. She really wanted to show this to Heather, to demonstrate what kind of person Chad was, if there was still doubt in Heather's mind.

And what had Chad done when he'd discovered that note? Had he gotten angry at Heather? Had he hurt her?

They had no way to contact her to find out.

Inside, Addie couldn't help looking around suspiciously at the living room. What had been a warm, lovely, familiar space with Chelsea's personality all over it in delightful eclectic touches suddenly felt dangerous, as if a threat could be lurking behind the formerly inviting furniture or around any corner.

She quickly collected Lucky's food, bed, and leash, and then stuffed her own things into the bag she'd brought for her stay.

Chelsea disappeared into her own room to grab some things and then darted into the bathroom.

Five minutes later, they were ready to leave.

Addie's heart felt so heavy as they walked away from the cottage. She couldn't imagine what was going through Chelsea's mind, having to flee the home she loved.

They followed Bennett, and Addie kept looking in the rearview, expecting to see someone tailing them. On the way, they skirted the block where Wild Rose Teas and Apothecary was located, which caused a painful little tug in the middle of Addie's chest.

Lucky jumped into the front seat, sitting sideways on her lap so he could look out the passenger window. He leaned his comforting warmth and weight against her, and she kissed the top of his soft head, so grateful nothing bad had happened to him.

They arrived in front of Bennett's house in an older but charming neighborhood northeast of downtown. Addie checked her phone as Chelsea turned off the lights and motor. It was after eleven.

"Oh gosh, it's late," Addie said ruefully. Her shoulders tensed as something occurred to her. "Were you planning to go to the boutique tomorrow?"

Chelsea shook her head. "I'm going to close the store for now."

Addie's heart sank to a new low. Not only had Aunt Kate been forced to temporarily shut down Wild Rose, but Chelsea was having to close Style.

"It's no big deal," Chelsea said. "Every so often I take a random day off. The store is more for fun than anything else."

Sometimes Addie forgot that Chelsea was basically a wealthy woman as a result of inheriting from her father when he'd passed away a few years back.

They wrangled their things and Lucky inside the pale stucco house with its steeply peaked roof, and the three of them stood blinking in the relative brightness of Bennett's living room. He glanced around, scratching his chin and shifting his weight, clearly self-conscious about having the two women there.

There was a gray microsuede sofa and matching recliner set up in the middle of the room, facing a TV mounted to the wall. The sofa looked almost brand new, but the easy chair showed signs of wear on the arms and the small table next to it held a remote, mug, and crumpled M&M package wrapper. A fireplace that looked like it never got used occupied a corner. And a desk with some mail, manilla folders, and a laptop took up a wall. There were black-and-white framed photographs of nature scenes on the wall behind the sofa.

Chelsea had her phone in her hand. "I'm going to call in the note." She walked toward the front door, gazing out the window as she pressed the phone to her ear.

Lucky trotted over to the sofa, jumped up, sat, and looked at them expectantly.

"Not on the furniture, boy," Addie said, pointing to the light-brown carpet and frowning. "That's not good manners."

Bennett waved a hand. "Aw, it's okay. He's a good dog, he can make himself at home. I was just thinking about how I hardly ever sit on that thing. I always seem to end up in the chair. Lucky might as well have at it."

He walked over with a faint smile and scratched Lucky behind an ear.

"Kind of nice to have a dog in the house," Bennett said quietly.

Chelsea finished the call and rejoined them. "Someone's going out to my place, and they're going to call me back."

Addie remembered how when she'd visited Bennett here before he hadn't asked her inside. He was a private person, and she'd respected it. But in the midst of the current emergency, she wondered exactly how uncomfortable it made him to have guests. Fortunately, Lucky's presumptuous claiming of the sofa seemed to have eased some of the tension. Bennett gave them a very quick tour—there were three bedrooms, one bathroom, and a kitchen with a dining area. One of the bedrooms housed a weight bench and a rack of hand weights, a small TV, and a treadmill. But the other spare room had a queen-sized bed that had some boxes stacked on it.

The whole house was relatively neat, if a bit spare.

The three of them reconverged in the living room.

"I'm really, really worried about Heather," Addie said, looking at Bennett. "We don't know her number or her address."

"I told the police Heather's connection to the note," Chelsea said. "But I don't know if it's enough for them to check on her."

"I'm going to double-check the doors and windows and make sure the property surveillance system is working properly," Bennett said. "And then I'll track down Heather's number so we contact her."

Addie nodded and wrapped her arms around her middle. She was glad to have a safe place to stay but had a sinking feeling that there was really no place to hide.

Chapter Twenty-One

AFTER BENNETT MADE SURE ALL the windows and doors were secure, he sat at his desk and opened his laptop. With Addie and Chelsea each looking over one of his shoulders, he showed them the live feeds from the cameras set up around the property. They had night vision and showed the quiet front, side, and back yards, plus the front door, back door, and a view from the house facing the alley.

"There are motion lights all around the house, too," he said.

Addie's shoulders eased a little bit.

"I want to keep the lights off, though," Bennett continued. "It'll make it easier for us to see anything outside."

And it would make for more difficult targets inside the house, too, Addie thought with a tiny shiver. She had to resist the urge to sidle away from the window the desk was set up under.

"Do you happen to have candles?" Chelsea asked. "We could light a few throughout the house to keep us from being in complete darkness."

"Sure, I've got some in case of electrical outage," he said.

Addie suppressed a small smile. Of course, that would be the only reason for practical, solve-any-problem Bennett Brooks to own candles.

"If you want to tell us where they are, we can grab them," Addie said. "That way you can get to work tracking down Heather's contact info."

He looked hesitant for a second but then said, "In the guest bedroom there's a dresser. Bottom drawer has some emergency supplies. The candles should be there."

"Great," Chelsea said. "We'll go around and make sure all the blinds are closed, and then we'll grab those candles."

Addie took care of the blinds in the three bedrooms while Chelsea took care of the bathroom and kitchen. Lucky trotted after Addie while she moved through the house.

Addie couldn't help checking out Bennett's bedroom with curiosity, but there really wasn't much to see. Neatly made bed against the wall with a navy duvet. There was only one nightstand. An antique chair with a creased leather seat and claw feet stood in a corner, with a duffel bag on it. The closet doors were closed.

Chelsea met Addie in the spare room, and she knelt to open the bottom dresser drawer.

"He's definitely prepared," Addie murmured as she took in an emergency radio, bottles of water, some squat white pillar candles, matches, and a couple of lighters. There was also a large first-aid kit. Lucky peered into the drawer, too, and sniffed the nearest items.

She took out three candles and one of the lighters and set them on top of the dresser.

"Maybe there are some spare sheets in here, too," Chelsea said, looking in the other drawers. After opening the middle of the five, she said, "Bingo, here we go."

She stacked some plain white sheets and a brown flannel blanket next to the candles.

They moved the boxes from the bed onto the floor and then quickly made up the bed.

Then Chelsea's phone jangled with a snippet of "Walking on Sunshine."

"Oh, that might be a detective," she said and answered it.

It was clear in the first few words she said that it was indeed someone from the police station.

Not wanting to make Chelsea uncomfortable by hovering while she was on the phone, Addie wandered into the living room with a candle and the lighter. She lit the wick and set the candle on the coffee table in front of the sofa. Lucky reclaimed his spot, with his head propped on the sofa's armrest.

"She's on the phone with the police. Any luck?" she asked, walking over to where Bennett was hunched over his laptop.

"I've got Heather's address, but I haven't yet tracked down a current cell phone number," he said. "It looks as if she may have been changing her number every year to eighteen months over the past few years."

Addie frowned. "That seems odd. It's such a pain to update your number when it changes."

Bennett pushed his chair around and then crossed his arms and looked up at her, rocking thoughtfully back and forth. The chair creaked softly.

"Well," he said. "In my experience, there are usually a couple of reasons people change their number. One, because they were in a relationship that went bad."

"But changing it several times?"

"That can mean debt collectors."

"Oh." Addie let out a breath. "You think she's had some financial trouble, huh?"

"Possibly, but that's not particularly relevant to the immediate problem."

"Well, we have her address. One of us could drive over there and check on her."

Bennett shook his head. "I don't want the three of us separated."

"We could all go together?" Addie suggested.

"Let's see what the police had to say to Chelsea. My hope is that they'll verify Heather's safety. If not, we may need to step in, and in that case, yes, I can drive all of us over there."

Lucky let out a soft whine from the sofa.

"You too, Lucky," Bennett said with a faint grin.

Addie went to sit down, and Lucky stood up, circled around twice, and then lay down with his chin resting on her thigh. She scratched the back of his neck, and he let out a contented sigh.

A minute or two later, Chelsea walked in. Addie's brows crept up expectantly.

"They took the note and knife as evidence," Chelsea said. "They're going to knock on Chad's door first thing in the morning."

"What about Heather?" Addie asked.

Chelsea pushed a wave of blond hair behind her ear and perched on the arm of the sofa.

"That was a little tricky," she said. "I couldn't really go into the whole Chad's-a-murderer thing because, you know, no solid proof. But I stressed the fact that the note was left on Heather's car because we believed she was in danger, and that Chad's reaction makes it pretty clear what he thought of that. So they're sending a patrol car over to Heather's house."

"Now?" Addie asked, her hopes lifting.

"Yes, within the hour."

"Oh, that's really good news," Addie said. She turned to Bennett, who'd remained still and quiet. "Don't you think?"

"I'm glad Heather is on their radar," he said with a slow nod. "But . . ."

Addie tilted her head. "What?"

"Would you ladies be up for a small stakeout?" he asked. "Lucky, too, of course."

"A stakeout?" Chelsea repeated, with a small, confused shake of her head.

"I want to go to Heather's and make sure the police do actually check on her, for one," Bennett said. "And if she's not there, we may need to swing by Chad's house."

"You have his address, too, I take it?" Addie asked.

Bennett nodded. "I know it's late. Are you sure you're up for it?"

"No, it's the right thing to do," she said. "I wouldn't be able to sleep worrying about her, anyway."

Not to mention worrying about whether Chad was going to come after them in the night. Addie felt relatively safe at Bennett's, but she couldn't help feeling anxious at the idea that there was a man out there who wanted to hurt her and Chelsea.

"Same here," Chelsea said, hugging her arms around her waist.

"Okay." Bennett stood. "We should head out."

Addie grabbed her purse and Lucky's leash, and they all met at the front door.

Her pulse tapped nervously as she opened the back door of Bennett's Jeep Sahara and waited for Lucky to jump in. She climbed in after him, and Chelsea took the front seat.

The car was tense and quiet as Bennett drove through the dark toward downtown. They ended up in an area Addie didn't know well that wasn't far from Highway 8, which skirted Stargaze.

After passing a trailer park and a gas station, Bennett turned into what appeared to be an old neighborhood with lots of towering pines.

"It's on Lancelot Road," he said.

The neighborhood's streets seemed to have been named in a Camelot theme: Galahad Street, Arthur Street, Knight Way, Merlin Road.

Some of the houses had been updated, but many looked original and most of those were dilapidated, with sagging fences, peeling paint, cracked driveways, and yards that needed weeding. Most of the homes were small, one story, and box shaped, with a few larger split-level houses here and there.

Bennett slowed to a crawl, checking the map on his phone. They were approaching a stop sign where the road teed off left and right. He pulled over short of the stop sign and pointed ahead.

"It's that one," he said, indicating a house that was past the stop sign and to the right.

It was one of the smaller houses, with overgrown grass in the front yard and dark windows. A screen door hung slightly askew, the front of the house weakly lit by a streetlight.

"If the police pull up there, they might block our view," Chelsea said.

"True," Bennett agreed. "I'll circle around and park on their street so we'll have a clear line of sight."

He made a left turn at the stop sign, flipped a U-turn at the next intersection, and then parked on the side of Lancelot Road about a half block from Heather's house. He killed the engine and the lights.

"She lives with her mother, right?" Addie asked.

"Looks like it from the records I dug up," Bennett said.

"I don't see her car," Addie said.

"Maybe there's an alley with a garage or carport in the back," Chelsea said.

"You know, I should have thought of that," Bennett said. "I was so focused on getting here before the police so we could observe what happens. I should have driven around to the back to check for a car."

"We could make a quick circle to see," Chelsea said.

Bennett seemed to hesitate. "We probably should. If she's not here, we need to see if she's at Chad's."

Just as he put his hand on the key, which was still in the ignition, a car pulled up to the stop sign.

"Wait, that's the patrol car," Addie said.

She scrunched down in the seat, and Bennett and Chelsea did the same. They watched the police cruiser turn right and then flip around to park in front of Heather's house.

An officer in uniform—a man—got out of the car and ambled up to the front door with a younger female officer at his side.

"Hey, that looks like Officer Davis," Addie whispered.

She wasn't sure why she was whispering; it wasn't like the officers could hear her. But it felt important to not attract attention.

They watched as Officer Davis pressed the buzzer, knocked, and then took a couple of steps back.

There was a flicker of curtains at the front window. A light illuminated inside.

The door opened, and a squat figure was silhouetted in the doorway.

"That's Edna on her scooter," Addie murmured.

It appeared a short conversation took place there in the doorway. It was too far for Addie to read Edna's expression, but the woman made a couple of sharp, irritated-looking gestures with her hands.

"Why isn't Heather coming to the door?" Chelsea whispered.

The door closed after a couple of minutes, the visit apparently over.

"No, no, don't leave. She needs help," Addie said under her breath, her heart sinking as she watched the officers get back into their car.

"They're probably going to be sitting there for a few minutes," Bennett said. "They may be trying to call Heather. They might be calling their superior to say they're going to Chad's."

"Can we go see if Heather's car is there?" Addie asked.

Nervous adrenalin was starting to pump through her. She had a terrible feeling that Heather was with Chad and she wasn't okay.

"Yes," Bennett said grimly. "Both of you stay down so the cops don't catch sight of you. I'm going to have to drive by them. I don't want to risk catching their attention by flipping a U-turn right in front of them."

Addie bent to the side, lying down on the seat. Chelsea slid down until Addie couldn't see her in the front seat.

Bennett started the car, pulled away, and drove forward. A moment later, he was making a left turn around Heather and Edna's block. He made another turn.

"I'm in the alley now," he said. "There's a carport and—" He cut off and whispered something under his breath.

After throwing the Jeep into park, he jumped out with the engine still running.

"What's going on?" Addie asked, alarmed. "What's wrong?"

She straightened.

Chelsea sat up too, and then she gasped.

"Wait, that's Heather's car," Addie said, squinting. "Oh no."

The driver's door to Heather's compact car was open, the dome light on. There were items strewn on the ground.

Addie got out and went to Bennett's side. He was leaning into the car but wasn't touching anything.

"What happened?" she asked.

"She left in a hurry," he said. "Or someone forced her to leave."

She surveyed the things on the ground: a couple of sodas, some cigarettes, a small bag of chips, and a pre-made sandwich. Toeing the white plastic bag, she saw a logo on it.

"That's the name of the gas station we drove past," she said. "It looks like Heather stopped there on her way home."

"You've worked with Officer Davis before, back when Kate was missing, right?" Bennett said quickly.

"Yes."

"Do you have his direct number?"

Addie started tapping her phone's screen. "Yep. Just sent it to you."

"I'm going to call him and tell him about this," Bennett said. "But I don't want the cops to see you here. I don't want to give them any indication you're chasing the killer whose crime you got blamed for."

"Okay," Addie said, nodding.

She felt numb and a little faint. Chelsea came to stand next to her.

"He must have come after Heather after he stabbed that note onto my door," Chelsea said, her voice low.

Bennett backed up, but then something seemed to catch his eye, and he leaned closer to the car. "I think that's blood." He pointed to a dark crimson splatter on the inside of the driver's window.

Addie's hands went cold. "Let's get in the car," she said to Chelsea. "I need to be gone from this scene before the police come to look."

They all quickly got back into the Jeep, and Bennett pulled away with his phone to his ear. "Hello, Officer Davis? This is Bennett Brooks. Someone asked me to check on Heather Schmidt. I just drove through the alley behind her house, and her car is there but the door is open and her groceries are spilled on the ground. There may be blood on the window."

He paused, and Addie couldn't hear the other end of the conversation.

"It's a private client, and I can't reveal who hired me," Bennett said into the phone. "I will tell you it's not Chad Caravelli, her boyfriend. But I have reason to believe he is very angry with her right now. I have his home address, and I can text it to you."

His eyes flicked to Addie's in the rearview. She knew he was trying to point the cops toward Chad without making any outright accusations that couldn't be backed up.

"Yes, I'll have my phone on me," Bennett said and then ended the call.

"Please tell me they're going to Chad's," Addie said.

"They wouldn't reveal something like that to me if they were, but I'm hoping they'll put the pieces together." He passed his phone to Chelsea. "Could you text Officer Davis Chad's address? I have it pulled up in the maps app."

"What now?" Addie asked.

"We're going to take a little ride to Chad's," Bennett said, his brow lowering in concentration as he glanced down at his phone and started navigation in his maps app.

Addie swallowed hard and sent out a prayer to the universe that they wouldn't be too late for Heather.

Chapter Twenty-Two

BENNETT SPED UP, GOING OVER the speed limit, and Addie's heart rate increased along with the Jeep.

"What are we going to do when we get there?" Addie asked.

"If we beat the police, I'm going to knock on the door," he said, his voice almost a growl. "Maybe knock it down, if Chad won't answer."

"Bennett, I don't think that's a good idea," Chelsea said, turning to look at him. "We don't know what kind of weapons he has, or—or what he might do."

Out of the corners of her eyes, she cast a glance back at Addie.

But Addie couldn't agree with Chelsea's caution. Chad Caravelli had killed two people, and Addie was sure he wouldn't hesitate to do away with her, too, since he knew he'd been found out.

And who knew what he'd been doing to Heather? From their interaction on the sidewalk outside Glazed, it was clear she didn't feel she could stand up to him.

Addie couldn't imagine just sitting outside Chad's house, waiting for the police to do something, while Heather might be inside, terrified . . . or worse.

"You can't be involved," Bennett said firmly, looking at Addie in the rearview mirror. "Your case is at stake. If you have any direct involvement with Chad, it will have negative blowback on you."

"I'm already accused of murder," Addie said wryly. "How much worse could it get?"

"I'm serious. You've got to stay in the car, no matter what. Keep out of sight of the authorities if at all possible. Please, Addie." His voice pitched lower and took on an almost desperate tone.

He was worried about her—very worried. She suddenly realized he'd been hiding the depth of his concern. This new understanding made her feel both warm inside and more fearful about her fate.

"Okay," she said. "You're right."

They were headed into a part of Stargaze that, ironically, wasn't too far from the hills where the Akidos had lived. Bennett came to a hard stop across from a brick two-story home.

Short trip up the hill from here to kill Kenneth Akido, Addie couldn't help thinking with a small shiver.

"Lock the doors," he said.

He reached for his gun but then seemed to think better of it and left it in the holster as he got out of the Jeep.

Addie watched him jog across the street to Chad's house and absently wondered how the pharmacist was able to afford a house that seemed out of range for someone in his profession.

"I have a bad feeling about this," Addie said.

"Yeah," Chelsea said faintly. "I really wish he'd leave this to the police. I want to help Heather, of course, but . . ." Her shoulders rose, and she seemed to pull into herself.

Bennett pounded on the door with the side of his fist and then stood to the side with his right hand on his holstered gun.

"Are you thinking about Chad's aura?"

Chelsea nodded. "It was really horrible. I didn't want to go into the full details after I saw it. I think I was trying not to think about just how dark it was."

While Bennett waited, Addie held her breath and watched, not even daring to blink.

What would she do if things went wrong? She had no weapons herself.

Lifting her phone so she could keep an eye on things at Chad's front door, Addie found Officer Davis in her contacts. Her thumb hovered over the call button.

But nothing was happening. No lights in the house. No twitch of blinds or curtains in a window. No movement of a shadow within.

"Do you think maybe they're not here?" Addie asked, frowning.

"That would be bad," Chelsea said. "Because if Chad doesn't have her here, where did he take her?"

After another minute or so, Bennett backed away from the house, looking up at it, and then turned and jogged quickly back to the Jeep.

"See any signs of life?" he asked as he slid behind the wheel.

"Nothing," Addie said, leaning forward between the seats. "Maybe no one is there."

Bennett looked at the house, which had a closed garage door to the right. "I'm going to try to see if there's a car in there."

"Need help?" Chelsea offered.

"If you wouldn't mind, I could hoist you up so you can get a look inside."

They got out and went across the street. When the motion light in the driveway lit it up like a spotlight, Addie winced. What if the neighbors were looking?

Bennett laced his fingers together, and Chelsea stepped up and peeked into the window. She jumped down a second later, shaking her head.

Back in the car, the three of them stared at the house.

"What now?" Addie asked.

"I'm not sure," Bennett said. "I suppose we should let the police do their check of the place. They should put out an alert for Chad's car when they figure out Heather isn't here. Let's go back to my place. I'll do some more digging into Chad's life and try to figure out where he might be."

The ride to Bennett's house was quiet and gloomy.

Addie held Lucky to her chest as they all piled through the front door and into the living room.

She felt helpless, wired, and exhausted all at once.

"Why don't the two of you rest?" Bennett suggested. "You're welcome to the living room or the guest room. I'm going to do some deep searches on Chad to see if there might be a relative's house or other property where he could be hiding out. I promise I'll let you know if I find anything or if the police get in touch."

There was absolutely no way Addie could sleep. She and Chelsea exchanged a look, and Addie saw her own fatigue and worry reflected in her friend's blue eyes.

"Mind if I turn on the TV?" Chelsea asked. "I'll keep the volume low."

"My TV is your TV," Bennett said. "And you're both welcome to anything you can find in the kitchen, too, no need to ask. You're welcome to rummage around."

That appeared quite a shift in Bennett's feelings about having people in his home, and it gave Addie a warm little spark of happiness.

"Thank you."

She smiled at Bennett, and their gazes met briefly. He smiled back before turning to his desk. Her attention shifted to Chelsea, who seemed to be trying to make herself small, curling into a ball on the sofa.

A memory from childhood summers surfaced in Addie's mind, the summer when they were fourteen, she thought it was. It was one of the rare times she spent the night at Chelsea's—usually they would stay at Aunt Kate's apartment or go camping—and Addie remembered being jealous that Chelsea had a big screen TV in her room. When it was time to go to sleep, they pulled the trundle bed out and cozied up on it under blankets. Chelsea had reached for the remote and cast Addie a look that seemed apologetic and a little embarrassed.

"I can't fall asleep without the TV on," she'd said quietly. "Is that okay?"

Chelsea had alluded to the nightmares that had plagued her childhood, and over the years Addie realized her friend found comfort in the flickering screen and old sitcom reruns, and they helped Chelsea ward off bad dreams enough to get to sleep.

Poor Chelsea. This is stressing her out more than she's letting on.

"I'm going to lay down in the guest room," Addie said.

She knew she wouldn't be able to sleep, but she needed to think.

On the queen bed with Lucky curled up against her side, she sent a text to Aunt Kate. It was very late—almost two in the morning—but Addie really wanted to hear her aunt's voice.

When there was no response, Addie nearly hit the call button with her thumb but then decided against it. The only reason to call Aunt Kate would be to see if she knew anything about Chad that might help; otherwise, Addie would only be causing her aunt more stress and angst, and there'd already been enough of that. Kate had done so much, and at the cost of having to close her store.

Addie set her phone on her chest, folded her hands across her lower belly, and took a deep breath.

Think . . . think.

She tried to relax and let her mind drift, hoping that calm would bring answers. Back when she'd worked in biotech and run into roadblocks in her lab work, she'd often found that a walk or a short, calming breathing exercise would bring clarity. It was really just about letting her head rest and drift.

Her muscles relaxed, and her mind followed. She nearly dozed, riding the edge between sleep and wakefulness. She started to dream of Aunt Kate's shop.

In the dream, there was a faint, airy whistle.

A teakettle.

Addie's eyes popped open, and she sat up.

"A tea-leaf reading," she whispered. "It couldn't hurt."

She tiptoed to the kitchen, glancing into the living room where Chelsea was huddled under a blanket. Bennett sat hunched over his laptop.

A quick look in the pantry revealed a box of Lipton tea bags. Bennett didn't have cups with matching saucers, so she found a small plate and a mug with the logo for the Seattle Seahawks football team on it. She filled the mug halfway with water and put it in the microwave for two minutes.

She hit "cancel" before the microwave could beep and pulled out the steaming mug.

Needing loose tea for the ritual, she cut open the Lipton bag with a steak knife from the block on the counter and dumped out the brown, flaky tea.

With the mug on the plate, she sat down, propped her elbows on the table, and looked into the water. Gradually, the tea saturated and began to sink. Faint curls of steam rose to caress her face. As she watched, she thought about Heather and tried to be patient with the process even while worry churned in her stomach.

Where are you, Heather?

After a minute or so, Addie realized she needed to bring Chad into her thoughts, too, as unpleasant as that was.

Where have you taken her?

Focusing on Heather, Chad, and the question of where they were at that moment, Addie started sipping once the tea leaves had sunk to the bottom of the mug. She drank until there was only a half inch or so of tea left.

The buzzing was already starting in the center of her chest and inside her skull. Breathing through the uncomfortable sensation, she kept her thoughts trained on Heather and Chad.

Her pulse sped as she turned the mug upside down onto the plate.

Dizziness swirled through her, seeming to scatter the buzzing throughout her body. Fighting the disorientation, she flipped the mug upright.

Her vision doubled and then blurred, and her breath came faster.

Indistinct whispering filled her mind.

"Please, just give me a clear answer," she murmured under her breath.

Looking down into the mug, she waited for it to come into focus.

She peered closer, frowning. Normally, the tea ran and clumped on the sides and even sometimes on the rim.

But this time, all of the soggy tea had stayed at the bottom of the mug. She tipped it slightly toward the light.

Strange.

It formed what appeared to be a squat arrow pointing up. And there were two distinct letters: Y and K.

Addie gasped. "Yuna and Kenneth."

And the arrow wasn't an arrow. It was a rudimentary shape of a house as if from a child's drawing, with a square base and a triangle roof.

She stood so swiftly she nearly knocked her chair backward. Catching it with her free hand as it wobbled, she set it on its feet. With the mug in her other hand, she hurried into the living room.

"They're at the Akido's house," she said.

Bennett swiveled around, and Chelsea sat up. Both of them stared at Addie.

She tried again. "Chad has Heather at Kenneth and Yuna's."

"The tea leaves told you?" Chelsea asked, her eyes flicking to the mug in Addie's hand.

She nodded. "Couldn't be more clear. And I can't believe I didn't think of it, actually."

Bennett was already on his feet and reaching for his keys. "I'm going to drive up there," he said. "And I'll call the cops on the way."

"We'll come, too," Addie said, looking around for her purse.

"I can't let you do that," Bennett said. "Please trust me; it's for your own good. Lock up right behind me."

"But—" Addie protested.

He was already running out the door.

Anger spiked through her chest. She turned to Chelsea, hands on hips.

"Let's follow him in your car."

"No, Addie," Chelsea said quietly. "He's right. You can't go anywhere near that house."

Addie threw her arms up in the air. It was a good thing there was no more liquid in the mug, because the motion would have sloshed soggy tea all over. "But Chad is dangerous! Bennett shouldn't be going alone."

"He knows what he's doing. And think about it, hon. That's the home of the person you're accused of killing. There's absolutely no way that goes well for you when the police show up."

Darn it all. Chelsea was right. Especially since Addie would have to appear in court in twelve hours.

"Okay," Addie said, slumping in defeat. "But let's get Bennett on video call. He can put us on mute. Then at least we'll be able to hear what's happening and get help if it goes wrong."

"That's a good idea," Chelsea said. "Why don't you do that? I need to lock the door."

She started untangling herself from the blanket. Addie had retrieved her phone from the guest bed and had just stepped into the living room when the front door swung open with force and rebounded off the wall. Chelsea was right there. Apparently she hadn't locked the door yet.

Chelsea screamed and Addie gasped as Chad Caravelli loomed in the doorway. A blade glinted in his hand.

He kicked the door closed with his heel and lunged for Chelsea.

Chapter Twenty-Three

ADDIE'S BRAIN SCREAMED AT HER to escape, to run out the back door and get help.

But she couldn't leave Chelsea alone with a killer.

"Let her go!" Addie screeched, racing forward.

Chelsea had tried to dart out of Chad's grasp, but he caught her hair in his fist. Yanking her back with one hand, he brandished the knife at Addie in the other.

"Stay there, or I'll slit her throat," Chad growled.

Addie stopped short and held out her hands as Chad pulled Chelsea to his chest, put her in a chokehold, and held the knife an inch from her neck.

Chelsea's blue eyes were huge, her face paper white, as her gaze locked on Addie.

"That's right, you stay right there," Chad said, his eyes dark with menace.

"Don't hurt her," Addie said. Her hands were shaking.

Behind Chad, the front door hadn't closed completely. A few inches of the dark night beyond showed between the door and the frame. But the lights in the living room were off, with only the flicker of the TV and the faint glow of Bennett's laptop screensaver to illuminate what was happening. It was unlikely someone outside would see and get help, especially at this hour.

Chad zeroed in on the phone in Addie's hand. "Throw that behind you! Throw it far. Do it now!"

She turned and tossed the phone toward the kitchen and heard it clatter on the wood floor.

"It's gone," Addie said, turning back around and showing him her empty hands.

Bennett would return. They just had to hang on until then.

A smirk twisted Chad's mouth. "I know what you're thinking, but he's not going to be back anytime soon."

Addie sucked in a breath, fearing the worst.

Chad shook his head. "I'm not that stupid. Just a couple of slow leaks in his tires. He'll get stuck far from here."

With his arm still locked around Chelsea's throat, he started moving forward.

She heard the soft tap of Lucky's paws on the kitchen floor. He'd come to investigate, but he was being sneaky about it.

Smart little dog.

But then a low rumbling growl came from the dark kitchen.

Chad's gaze skipped past Addie.

She turned her head slightly. "Lucky, *go*. Out the front door," she whispered. "Get help."

Was she really telling a little brown poodle mix to alert someone they were in trouble? Logic told her it was ridiculous, but she knew in her gut Lucky understood what she was saying.

"Is someone else back there?" Chad demanded.

Just then, Lucky burst from the dark kitchen, running at top speed. As he raced past, he snarled and nipped at Chad's ankle. Lucky squeezed through the door opening and disappeared out into the night.

It was too much to hope that he would find Bennett, but maybe Lucky would be able to help somehow. If nothing else, at least he was safe.

Chad swore and twisted to look at his ankle—apparently Lucky's teeth had found skin.

"Stinking mutt," Chad muttered under his breath. To Addie, he said, "You, stay right where you are. If you make a move, your friend's dead. Got it? Nod to tell me you got it."

Addie nodded.

He dragged Chelsea backward, shouldered the door closed, and used his knife hand to clumsily lock the deadbolt.

Then he was striding toward Addie with the knife once again at Chelsea's neck.

"Go," he snapped at Addie. "Kitchen. Turn the light on."

"Addie, run out the back," Chelsea breathed.

"You do that, and she's dead," Chad said to Addie.

With an ugly look that might have been a smile or a grimace, he touched the blade to Chelsea's throat. A bead of blood formed.

Chelsea looked absolutely terrified.

Addie froze. "I won't, I won't. I won't do anything. Please, just don't hurt her." Her voice took on a pleading, desperate tone she'd never heard from her own mouth before.

This man had already killed two people, possibly Heather, too. He knew Addie and Chelsea had discovered he'd killed the Akidos. Whatever he had planned, it probably didn't involve letting the women live.

Addie had no idea what to do. She'd never been so scared in her life. But she couldn't just let this happen.

"Kitchen! Light!" Chad barked.

As she shuffled into the kitchen, she started to reach for the light switch when her toe bumped something. Her phone. She pretended to stumble and picked it up and slipped it into her back pocket. Then she flipped the light on.

"Pull that chair away from the table and sit down facing me," Chad commanded.

Addie did it.

He released the chokehold on Chelsea to pull something from his back pocket. It was a pack of zip ties, the extra-long ones. He pushed it into her hand and then shoved her forward.

"Zip her hands together and then do her legs to the chair," Chad said, coming up behind Chelsea's to peer over her shoulder. "Do it tight. I'm gonna check your work."

Addie's heart nearly broke when she saw the tears leaking down her friend's face.

After trying to send some silent strength to her friend, Addie looked up at Chad.

"Did you kill Heather, too?" Addie asked quietly.

Their only hope was to stall him and whatever he had planned until Bennett could get back.

"Shut up," he said, and Chelsea let out a soft squeak and stiffened. Chad must have jabbed the knife in her back.

"There's no need for that." Addie kept her voice low. "I just want to understand why you—you hurt people."

"I said shut it!" Chad said, clearly annoyed.

Chelsea finished with the zip ties, and then Chad ordered her into a chair and gave her the same treatment. She sat next to Addie, trembling and crying noiselessly.

"Why kill Yuna?" Addie asked. "What did she do to you?"

Chad huffed an exasperated breath. He took two more zip ties from the pack and put them in his mouth, and then he pulled one of Addie's elbows back against the chair back's post and looped the tie around her arm and through the chair. He pulled it so tight she ground her teeth against the pain. He did the same to her other arm and then to Chelsea's two arms.

Their wrists were bound, and their upper arms were tied to the chairs. Addie's upper body was basically immobilized.

He eyed them. "Don't try anything. I'll be right back."

Then he disappeared into the living room, and a moment later Addie heard the front door open and then close.

She could start screaming, but the lots in this neighborhood were wide. It was unlikely a neighbor would hear.

But she had her phone.

She started scooting around.

"My phone is in my back pocket. Do you think you can reach it?"

"I'll try," Chelsea said.

Addie painstakingly maneuvered her chair so her hip was next to Chelsea's thigh. They leaned toward each other, pulling against their restraints.

There was the sound of a siren in the distance, and for a second Addie's heart leapt. But the noise faded away instead of coming closer.

"Addie, he's going to kill us," Chelsea said, her voice shaking.

"No, he's not," Addie said firmly.

"His aura." Chelsea sobbed. "It's, oh, it's so dark."

"Just focus on the phone," Addie said soothingly. "If you can get it, put it into my hand."

"I got it."

Addie shoved backward until their bound hands were even and then twisted as hard as she could to reach and grasp the phone with her fingers.

She clumsily started trying to navigate the screen. She managed to enter the code to unlock the phone when there was a noise at the front door.

No time to make a call.

Addie pressed one of the buttons on the side of the phone and held it. She'd programmed that button to start her voice recorder, which she used to use all the time when she was working in the lab and wanted to be able to record notes about her experiments without having to stop to write or type.

She shoved the phone in between her thighs just as Chad appeared in the kitchen's doorway.

He was slightly out of breath, and he was holding a large red plastic container.

The blood froze in Addie's veins.

It was a gas can. He was going to light the place on fire.

Anger suddenly burned away her fear. She'd tried being compliant and soothing, and it hadn't worked. Time for a different approach.

She scoffed. "You know what? You're a sad excuse for a man. You control and manipulate Heather, and then you barge in here and tie up two defenseless women. You're pathetic."

Chad squinted at her and cocked his head. "Keep talking, honey. Enjoy it while you still can."

"You're weak," Addie spat. "You killed Yuna on accident because—because you're not only evil, you're . . . you're terrible at your job."

He let out a bark of a laugh. "Well, I did get the wrong person, so maybe I am terrible at my job." He laughed again.

He wasn't looking at her. He was pulling the lid off the end of the gas can's spout.

Addie's heart tried to jump up her throat.

"Were you trying to kill Kenneth?" she asked.

"Nah, I was aiming to get rid of the old lady."

He lifted the plastic can, grunting and lugging it closer to the women. When he set it down, a bit of gas splashed out, the fumes quickly permeating the air.

"What old lady?" Addie asked. Her eyes widened. "You mean Edna, don't you?"

Shaking his head, he snorted. "Yeah, I screwed that one up pretty good, I guess. Edna was supposed to get the fentanyl in place of one of her usual meds. The old biddy is on about a hundred of them. I wasn't paying attention, and the pill bottles got mixed up. Kenneth Akido ended up with the fentanyl meant for Edna. Oops!" He gave an exaggerated shrug.

Chad tipped the can and gas spilled over Addie's feet, saturating her socks and the lower few inches of her pant legs with cold liquid.

"It was a good plan, if I hadn't messed up. Once Edna was gone, Heather could collect the life insurances. She's got two juicy policies on her mother because they're not only family but business partners too." He began making a slow circle around Addie and Chelsea, spilling gas and splashing them as he went. "So with the old lady gone, I'd, you know, comfort poor Heather in her time of pain. Ask her to marry me. Probably also convince her to sell her donut place because the memories of the place would just be too painful. We'd have a shotgun wedding, I'd get myself on her bank accounts, and then I'd have full access to the cash."

The fumes were making Addie's head swim and her eyes water. Her throat rebelled, and she started coughing.

"That plan is obviously shot. Now it's clean-up time. I've just got to make sure I've taken care of everyone who could cause me trouble." He moved in front of them and straightened, still holding the gas can. "It's okay, though. I've had to start from square one before. I'll figure it out."

With a firm nod, he tipped the can and started backing toward the rear of the house in the direction of the back door. He was making a trail of fuel.

"He's going to light up this house and run," Chelsea said, gagging on the fumes.

Their feet were in a puddle of gas, and more of it had wicked up from Addie's socks to her pants, reaching nearly to her knees. But worse, the air was so saturated with gas fumes, she was afraid a spark just might cause an explosion that would blow the roof off—and Addie and Chelsea to pieces.

"Try to get to the hallway," Addie said to Chelsea. Addie began shifting her weight, pushing the chair and rocking it to try to move across the floor. "The gas probably hasn't soaked onto the carpet yet!"

Chelsea began scooting, too.

Addie glanced toward the back door and saw it open. Chad stood outside, illuminated by light spilling from the kitchen. He put the gas can down and dug in his pocket, producing a lighter.

"Go!" Addie screamed to Chelsea.

They were barely making any progress across the kitchen floor, and Addie was so light-headed from fumes she was afraid she might pass out.

As if in a dream, she watched over her shoulder as Chad flicked his thumb over the igniter mechanism. The lighter sparked but didn't catch.

He tried again, and a flame appeared.

Looking up, he gave her a little wave. Then he leaned over, ready to drop the lighter into the gas spilled in front of him.

Cold despair filled Addie. This was it. She and Chelsea were going to be burned alive.

She started screaming as loud as she could with a last-ditch hope that someone—anyone—would hear through the open back door.

Chapter Twenty-Four

ADDIE'S HEAD POUNDED WITH THE sound of her own screams, as if her voice was pressurizing the inside of her skull.

She watched the flame on Chad's lighter.

But before he could drop it into the puddle of fuel, there was a blur of motion behind him.

Another sound cut through Addie's screams.

Was that . . . Lucky?

The little dog was barking and snarling furiously, lunging in from behind to snap at Chad's legs.

Chad straightened and twisted around, momentarily forgetting the lighter. The flame went out. He waved his arms at Lucky, shouting at the dog.

Run, boy, save yourself.

Chad turned back to his lighter, flicked it, and the flame reappeared.

And then he was flying to the side and out of sight.

Addie paused in her scooting scramble. She stared at the back door, seeing only Lucky there. "Where did Chad go?"

Then a shot rang out. There was shouting.

And then chaos, as sirens wailed, speeding their way until the sound was almost deafening.

Addie heard the front door burst open. And someone ran in through the back, sliding to a stop on the puddle of fuel in the kitchen. It was Bennett.

"I got him. I got him," he was saying.

Addie just stared, not understanding.

People in uniform were storming in through the front of the house. They converged in the kitchen. Bennett spoke to them briefly, directing them out through the back.

"Here," he said, kneeling next to Addie. He pulled out a pocketknife and began cutting away the zip ties.

Her ankles and arms were free. She tried to stand, but her legs were too wobbly. With both ends of the house open, fresh air breezed through. She sucked in deep breaths and watched in a daze as Bennett cut Chelsea free.

Addie remembered her phone. She reached under her and stopped the voice recording. Then she held the phone up.

"I got Chad's confession," she said.

He offered his hand to help Chelsea to her feet, but his eyes were on Addie. "You—what?"

"I recorded him confessing." Addie said. She hit play on the audio file and turned up the volume.

It was a little muffled, but Chad's voice and words were clear.

Bennett stared at her. "You're incredible. I can't believe you got this."

Officer Davis and Detective McCann walked in just as Chad was describing how he'd intended to kill Edna but accidentally killed Yuna instead.

Detective McCann blinked, and her mouth fell open. "Is that . . . ?"

"It's Chad Caravelli's confession," Addie said. "He killed Yuna and Kenneth Akido. He just tried to kill us." She turned to Bennett. "Heather?"

"She's alive," Bennett said.

Addie slumped in relief. "Oh, thank goodness. Where's Chad?"

Bennett pointed with his thumb over his shoulder. "Out back. He's got a gunshot wound in his leg, courtesy of me. I zip-tied him to my patio table. It's got a cement block, so he's not going anywhere."

Feeling strong enough to stand, she got to her feet and went to Chelsea, enveloping her trembling friend in a hug. Addie said soothing things into Chelsea's hair, and they hung on to each other for a long moment.

Detective McCann, to her credit, waited patiently. "We need to get you some medical attention," she said gently when Addie stepped back. "There's an ambulance out front."

"I need to get my dog first," Addie said. "Go ahead, Chels, I'm right behind you."

"Could I get your phone, Ms. James?" McCann asked.

Addie passed the phone to the detective. "Do you know if anyone has called my aunt?"

"Officer Davis did, I believe."

"Thank you." Addie made her way carefully out of the kitchen to the back yard.

Lucky had been waiting in the back yard, letting out little yips and whines. He badly wanted to come to her, she could tell, but he seemed to not want to walk through the gas.

Once she was clear of the fuel, Lucky took a short running start and leaped into her arms. She caught him, hugged him to her chest, buried her face in his fur, and sobbed for a few seconds. He gleefully wiggled around, trying to lick her cheeks.

"Brave boy," she whispered, kissing his soft head.

Then she turned to watch as Chad Caravelli was cut free from Bennett's table, hauled to his feet, cuffed, and read his rights. Officers marched him around the side of the house, paying no attention to Chad's cries and moans as he was forced to walk on a leg with a bullet in it.

Addie trailed behind and felt no pity for the man's pain.

The front of the house was a mess of vehicles—several police cars, a fire truck, and an ambulance where Chelsea sat in the open back with an oxygen mask on her face and a blanket around her shoulders.

With Lucky still in her arms, Addie went to join her friend. Addie got an oxygen mask and a blanket, too.

Chad was hollering for medical help, but the EMTs ignored him.

"He can wait for the next ambulance," said one of them, a stocky young man in his early twenties. He gave Chelsea a wink.

Then someone was running through the chaos calling Addie's name.

Aunt Kate.

She raced to Addie and Chelsea and threw her arms around both of them. Hank was right behind her, and he joined in, too.

Aunt Kate pulled back, tears spilling from her eyes as she shook her head. "Are you okay?"

Addie nodded. "Just soaked with gas and dizzy from the fumes." Her words were slightly garbled due to the oxygen mask. "He confessed, Aunt Kate. I got his confession on my voice recorder."

"Oh, what a miracle," Aunt Kate said, coming in for another embrace.

Addie smiled weakly.

They all turned to look as another ambulance zoomed up. Chad, along with two officers, was loaded into the back and taken away.

Addie and Chelsea looked at each other.

"I don't usually have these kinds of sentiments, but I hope he never sees the world again, except through prison bars," Chelsea said quietly.

Sadness gripped Addie's heart, because it *was* so unlike Chelsea to say such a thing. But it was unrealistic to expect this experience wouldn't change them.

"I agree," Addie said firmly.

"Do you need to take them to the hospital?" Hank asked the muscular EMT.

"Let us check their vitals and ask them a few questions," the EMT. "They may not need to."

He and the other EMT, a woman with a gray-streaked braid, quickly did their tests and asked Addie and Chelsea about their symptoms. The medical professionals concluded it was up to the women whether they felt good enough to go home.

"Aside from a slight headache, I think I'm okay," Addie said.

"Me, too," Chelsea agreed. "We need to change clothes, and I want to take a long shower. I'm afraid I'll never get the gas smell off."

The male EMT offered a sheet of paper with counseling resources. "You experienced something terrible tonight. There are people who can help you process the trauma."

"Thank you," Addie said.

Aunt Kate took the paper since Addie's hands were still full with Lucky, who seemed quite content to stay in her arms.

Detective McCann had been lurking near the ambulance, and she strode forward as soon as Addie and Chelsea relinquished their oxygen masks and stepped away from the ambulance.

"I know it's been a rough night," the detective said, pushing her curly red hair back from her forehead. "But we need to get statements from both of you about what happened. We can do it at the same time to speed things up."

Addie pulled the blanket tighter around her. "Do we have to go to the station?"

"No, wherever you're comfortable."

"I'd rather just get it over with now, if we can," Chelsea said.

"Of course. If you want to come with me, and then Ms. James can give her statement to Detective Malinas."

Addie went with the other detective, a man of about thirty with tan skin and quick eyes that were so dark they were nearly black.

When she was done, she caught Bennett's eye. He was talking to a couple of officers, but he lifted a hand and his gaze stayed on her as Aunt Kate bundled Addie and Chelsea into Kate's Subaru.

After, Hank drove all of them, and he and Aunt Kate stayed at Chelsea's house "just to make sure they didn't need anything."

By the time Addie and Chelsea had bathed and changed into clean clothes, the first light of day was starting to leak into the sky.

They both slept in Chelsea's bed with the TV on mute, flickering from the wall.

It was the sound of voices in the living room that roused Addie many hours later. She slipped from the bed, and Lucky hopped down to the floor on soft feet and followed her out.

Bennett was in the living room talking to Kate and Hank.

"Hi," Addie said, pulling the pink sweatshirt she'd borrowed from Chelsea tighter around herself.

"How are you doing?" he asked softly. "That was quite an ordeal."

All three of them were looking at Addie as if she might burst into tears at any moment, but actually she felt surprisingly calm.

"I'm doing okay," she said, coming to perch on the sofa arm. "It was a nightmare, and I truly thought we were going to die. But now I know Chad is going to pay for what he did, and that feels kind of good. Satisfying. How are you doing?"

"Oh, I'm fine," Bennett said, waving a hand. "The house is a mess, but that's what insurance is for."

"I'm so sorry," Addie said. "The gas probably destroyed the floor in the kitchen. Will you ever be able to get the smell out?"

"It'll get taken care of; I'm not worried," he said with a warm smile.

"Thank you for getting there when you did," Addie said. "If not for you . . ."

"Lucky helped," Bennett said.

They all looked at the little dog, who wagged at the sound of his name. He went to sit at Bennett's feet, twisting to look up at the man until he reached down to scratch the back of Lucky's neck.

"Thank you, Bennett, and thank you Lucky," Aunt Kate said, tearing up. She rose and came to Addie for a hug. "I'm so sorry for what you had to go through," she whispered.

"I'll be fine," Addie whispered back.

"Oh, I've got something for you." Bennett pulled something from the pocket of his light jacket.

"My phone!" Addie grinned and went to get the device. "I was afraid it'd get filed away as evidence and I'd never get it back. Worth it, if what's on it puts Chad away for good, but still."

"They took the audio file and the information they needed," Bennett assured her.

"I got a call from Maureen," Aunt Kate said. "She handled your court appearance, and things are already in motion to get your charges dropped. She's greasing the wheels, and she thinks it will only be a couple of days."

Addie clasped her hands at her chest, closed her eyes, and let out an enormous breath. "That may be the best news I've ever heard."

"Me too!" Chelsea said behind her.

She came to wrap her arm around Addie's waist.

Addie looked around at the people in the room as a lump formed in her throat.

"You all deserve more thanks than I can ever put into words," she said. "Thank you for supporting me in every way. Thank you for standing by me. I'm so sorry you had to close the shop for a while, Aunt Kate. Bennett, I feel so bad about what happened to your poor house. And Chelsea, I nearly—nearly got you . . ." Addie couldn't finish the sentence.

"No, you didn't," Chelsea said firmly. "*You* didn't do *anything* wrong."

"Well . . . thank you all so much," Addie said when she was able to take a breath to speak.

"Of course, dear," Aunt Kate said. She stood. "If you girls don't need anything from us, Hank and I are going to head out." Her eyes sparkled. "We've got to get the store ready to reopen!"

Addie brightened. "Really?"

Kate nodded. "And you'll be able to move back in soon."

THREE DAYS LATER, ADDIE WAS getting dressed for the day in the apartment above Wild Rose Teas and Apothecary after spending her first night back there. She was a free woman, cleared of all accusations, and Chad Caravelli had been charged with a long list of crimes.

Aunt Kate, who was making some strides in her adjustments to living as a Shuffler and understanding more and more about her own urges and needs, had worked a full shift on her own the day before. Since Addie was allowed back in the shop, she wanted to return to her former role, but she was nervous about whether customers would trust her. It would be good to have Kate there to help smooth the way.

Kate was already bustling around in the store when Addie went downstairs with Lucky, unlocking the front door and putting up the Open sign.

Someone was waiting outside.

"Heather, come in," Kate said, holding the door open.

"Hi," Heather said, her gaze skipping to the back of the store where Addie stood. "Oh, I'm so glad you're here. I wanted to talk to you."

"Are you all right?" Addie asked as Heather approached. "Bennett said Chad had you tied up at the Akido's house. That must have been terrifying."

Heather's face tightened, and she looked down. "It was. But I'm alive, and so are you. And Chad will never hurt anyone again."

Sympathy panged in the center of Addie's chest as she took in Heather's haunted expression.

"I wanted to thank you for offering to help me," Heather said. She shook her head, and her fluffy strawberry-blond hair floated around her shoulders as her eyes filled. "It almost cost you and Chelsea your lives."

Addie suddenly remembered the whispered words: Love and money. Chad had used Heather's love to try to steal her money. He didn't care about her, though. Money was his love.

"We're okay, though," Addie said, placing her hand on Heather's arm. "And so are you."

"Maybe I will be someday." Heather wiped tears from under her eyes. "I just hope you can forgive me."

"Of course, you are forgiven. I know Chels feels the same way."

Heather nodded. "Thank you." She turned and quietly left.

As the day passed, many people stopped by to see how Addie was doing—Betty and Octavia and Renaldo from the salon. Even Raj, Lisette's husband, dropped off a box of croissants, though he clearly felt a bit awkward about being at Wild Rose and didn't linger.

Trey paid a visit, too. He said something about getting together soon, but they didn't make any specific plans. And Addie realized she was okay with that. She'd had fun on their date but didn't think she had serious feelings for him. Or maybe she'd just been too scared and exhausted to clearly focus on that area of her life. Either way, she wasn't going to worry about it.

Addie was hugely relieved that there was a trickle of customers. She hung back, though, and let Kate wait on them, not sure the people of Stargaze would trust Addie to make their remedies.

Just before closing, Bennett came in.

When Aunt Kate saw him walk toward the counter, she waved, scooted to the back, and busied herself with something.

"Hi," Bennett said with a warm smile, though his dark eyes darted a little nervously.

"Hi," Addie said. "How are you?"

"Good, good." He nodded.

Addie peered at him. He was being a little weird.

"I, uh, wanted to ask you something," he said. He reached up and scratched his chin and then stuffed his hands into the front pockets of his jeans.

Addie tilted her head. "Oh?"

"Can I take you to dinner this weekend? I know this great little Italian place in Portland, if you're up for a bit of a drive."

Aunt Kate had been right! How had she known Bennett was going to ask Addie out?

"Yes, I'd love that," Addie said with no hesitation.

She'd gone out with Trey and truly enjoyed him and their kiss, but it wasn't anything exclusive. Plus, the thought of getting away from Stargaze with Bennett for an evening sounded like a dream.

"Oh, that's great," Bennett said, a genuine smile brightening his face.

He seemed to relax a little as they made arrangements.

As he walked out, Addie leaned against the counter and let out a long breath.

Aunt Kate came to the counter. "So . . . ?" she asked expectantly.

"Dinner," Addie said. She gave her aunt a sheepish smile. "You were right."

Kate grinned back. "That's wonderful news. He told me your magic saved Heather," she said.

Addie nodded. "I guess that's true. I'd almost forgotten."

"You have quite a talent, Addie." Aunt Kate smiled broadly. "And you're in just the right place to nurture it and see it flourish."

Addie gave a small nod. She was glad her tea-leaf readings had helped put a murderer away and save a woman's life.

Maybe she would decide to explore her powers more. She vowed to check out the book on tasseomancy Betty had given her. But for the moment, she was just grateful to go back to normal everyday life and savor her freedom.

In Addie's next magical mystery, *Chamomile and Crystal Balls*, the Apple Festival kicks off the fall festival season in Stargaze, and that means colorful trees, cozy coats, apple cider, and fun! It also means an influx of tourists, including a stranger from Betty's past. It turns out the palm reader has a secret past, and it's coming back to haunt her.

When a body turns up in Betty's fortuneteller tent at the Apple Festival, she becomes the prime suspect in the killing. She claims she's innocent, but her connection to the deceased only makes her appear more guilty.

Addie is determined to clear Betty's name. But is Addie's magic strong enough to do the job?

Chamomile and Crystal Balls by Thora Bluestone is now available!

Go to www.Thoraluestone.com/newsletter to sign up for subscriber-only updates, deals, freebies, and news from Thora!

Books by Thora Bluestone

The Tea Shop Witch Cozy Mysteries

The Tea Shop Witch (#1)

Peppermint and Potions (#2)

Chamomile and Crystal Balls (#3)

Bergamot and Brains (#4)

Vanilla and Vampires (#5)

www.ingramcontent.com/pod-product-compliance
Lightning Source LLC
Chambersburg PA
CBHW030138180626
46812CB00002B/748